Praise for C

"[*Percy's Field* is] beautifully written, sprinkled with sarcasm ... The magic comes from Brookhouse's evocative prose: 'The air was full of the damp traces that linger in old Southern houses, the smell of paper and fabric and wood and all the artifacts bequeathed generation to generation.'"

— Kirkus Reviews —

"Brookhouse's writing is so good and so elegant ... [*Percy's Field*] is not a fast-paced thriller that emphasizes action. Rather, this novel moves slowly in the Carolina humidity, and the emphasis is placed on the immaculate prose and the deep characterization given to Harr County and North Carolina's tobacco country. ... The book excels at presenting a dark and enjoyable murder story that resonates with the truth that the past is never really over."

— from a Foreword Clarion Review —

"*FINN* is the real thing—a southern Gothic tale in which the narrator must solve the mystery of his own nature in order to escape the web of violence in which he is caught. Start it when you have time to finish because you won't want to put it down."

— Terry Roberts, author of
A Short Time to Stay Here and winner of the
Willie Morris Award for Southern Fiction

"[*Silence*] is a quiet novel of personal and seasonal challenges set in a small town in New Hampshire. Brookhouse writes confidently and unobtrusively about authentic issues."

— Kirkus Reviews —

"Christopher Brookhouse has produced another literary wonder in *Old-Timer*. It is both easy to read and playfully complex."

— Rob Neufeld —
Asheville Citizen-Times

A Mind *of* Winter

CHRISTOPHER BROOKHOUSE

 Safe Harbor Books
Asheville, N.C.

Christopher Brookhouse
Safe Harbor Books
1 Page Avenue, #404
Asheville, NC 28801

ISBN: 978-0-9978686-6-1 (print)

ISBN: 978-0-9978686-7-8 (ebook)

Library of Congress Cataloging-in-Publication Data

Names: Brookhouse, Christopher, 1938- author.
Title: A mind of winter / Christopher Brookhouse.
Description: First Edition. | Asheville, N.C. : Safe Harbor Books, [2020] |
    Series: Gus salt series; 4 | Summary: "In this final installment of the
    Gus Salt series, the sheriff of Harr County, North Carolina, meets up
    again with the scofflaw Hunt brother as he searches for the identity of
    a burned body and the whereabouts of a missing woman, who seems
    connected to tragic events far beyond Harr County's borders. It's a cold
    and gloomy January, no solace for Gus in his own personal winter of
    discontent"-- Provided by publisher.
Identifiers: LCCN 2019052775 (print) | LCCN 2019052776 (ebook) | ISBN
    9780997868661 (trade paperback) | ISBN 9780997868678 (ebook)
Subjects: GSAFD: Suspense fiction.
Classification: LCC PS3552.R658 M56 2020 (print) | LCC PS3552.R658
    (ebook) | DDC 813/.54--dc23
LC record available at https://lccn.loc.gov/2019052775
LC ebook record available at https://lccn.loc.gov/2019052776

Cover image courtesy of A.Y. Smyth

Printed in the United States

Safe Harbor Books
www.safeharborbooks.com

For A.P.

A Mind *of* Winter

One must have a mind of winter
To regard the frost and the boughs
Of the pine-trees crusted with snow

I

Tuesday. A gray dawn breaking.

January 6. Epiphany, Gus remembered. He stood in the doorway of the sheriff's office and watched Zeno Wooten make his way from Bowen's diner, stepping carefully along the slippery sidewalk.

"How cold do you think it is?" Zeno asked, scuffing his boots on the doormat.

"The radio said twenty degrees."

"Christmas was sixty."

"That was too warm."

"Twenty is too damn cold."

"I agree." Gus moved aside. "Come in and get warm. Coffee's about ready."

"Don't need any. Drank three cups at the diner."

Zeno closed the door and followed Gus down the narrow hall to the office, pausing to notice a familiar face on one of the wanted posters pinned to the corkboard.

"Mr. Ware takes a fine picture," Zeno said. He shrugged off his coat. "I treated him for a strep infection."

"Felt well enough to rob a bank in Wake County and another in Orange County."

"Banks there have more to steal than what's here in Harr County. You've been sheriff for almost sixteen years, was our bank ever robbed? Can't remember."

"Once, before you came back from service. Nineteen forty-four. A gentleman from South Carolina. His girlfriend ran their getaway car off the road, and they surrendered to a state trooper."

Zeno sat down and watched Gus fill his coffee cup and spoon sugar into it. "Maggie said you liked it sweet."

"How is she?"

"Still thinks you took advantage of her."

"I think we took advantage of each other."

"I suppose that's what she and I are doing. She's a competent nurse though."

Gus looked at his watch. "You opening the clinic this morning?"

"I told Maggie to line people up and I'd be there at nine thirty — winter hours. Too much black ice to open earlier, like this morning."

"You ever get tired of doctoring?"

"Gus, bone-tired. This winter everyone seems to be falling sick."

"How's Neva?"

Zeno rubbed his hands together and looked around the room: the empty desk that the deputies shared, the pale cactus on the table beside the hot plate and coffeepot, the smiling photograph of President Eisenhower on the gray wall beside the office-size American flag, the filing cabinet, the gun lockup, the dark wooden chair that matched the one he was sitting in.

"Neva's got a new man," Zeno said.

"And how's that with you?"

"He makes her happy."

Gus pushed away from his desk, stood up, and moved the cactus from one side of the table to the other. He leaned against the wall and studied Zeno. The men had never been close, not because years earlier Gus, briefly, had been one of Neva's lovers but because they were each private people who didn't share their feelings, only their opinions. They respected each other, however, and were concerned for each other. Zeno appeared exhausted. As he said, bone-tired.

"It doesn't make you happy or you wouldn't be here," Gus said.

"I have no right to complain."

"You met him?"

"Seen him. You probably have too. He paints. Goes around the countryside, field and forest. Not that there are many trees left in Harr County with all the farming going on. Tobacco is a nasty crop, even if I partake. Sorry it's so profitable."

"What's his name?"

"Anthony Crim. Called Tony. Neva says he's a good painter. His father owned a gallery in Paris before the war."

"Age?"

"Forty something."

"He can afford to paint and not do other work?"

"Apparently. And play nymph and satyr when Neva's in the mood for it."

Gus picked up his cup. His coffee was cold now. "Forty's too young for a satyr, I think."

"Neva's forty-three, too old for a nymph, but I'm not going to tell her that."

"How old was Neva when you married her?"

"Twenty-five. What's your point?"

"We need to sow our wild oats sometime."

"Like I said, I can't complain, can I?

"So why are you here?"

"Yes, I almost forgot. Last night I was driving back from Kingsville and saw the Hunt brothers parked on the bridge. I slowed and passed and looked back in the mirror and saw one of them throw a bundle of some sort into the river. Knowing your opinion of them, I thought you might be interested."

"I am," Gus said.

Zeno stood and buttoned his coat. "By the way, driving here this morning, I saw a car in the ditch on the Ruffin Road."

"Usually someone would have reported it by now."

"Folks with any sense are staying home." Zeno picked up the book lying next to the phone on the deputies' desk and read the title. "*Selected American Poetry*? Which deputy is reading this?"

"Travis."

"I'm shocked. I've never seen him read anything except comic books."

"I was surprised too, but Miss Tolley got him interested in the poetry group she started."

"What's come over him?"

"He says he wants to improve himself. He plans to run for sheriff in the spring when I retire."

"You really going to do that?"

"I said I would."

"Then what?"

Gus shrugged. "Law school, maybe."

"They take people your age?"

"The university said I could apply."

"You saved anything?"

"Money, you mean?"

"Yes, money."

"Not much."

Zeno shook his head. "You need to learn from Blossom Hall and write yourself a book that sells like hers and becomes a movie."

"I gave up writing a long time ago."

"What about you and her?"

"What about your clinic? Considering the road conditions, don't you think you'd better be on your way?"

"I'll tell Maggie you asked after her," Zeno said. "Tell her you're concerned about her welfare."

"I'm concerned about everyone who lives in the county."

On the way to his car Zeno tried to remember the name of the magazine Maggie had found in the waiting room, a fan magazine a patient had left at the clinic. There was a photo of Blossom and a handsome young actor, the two of them holding hands. Neva predicted Blossom would sell lots of books, give up writing, and become an actress famous for her sex appeal, like her writing. She'd be on the cover of *Life* or *Time*. Zeno supposed the publication Maggie had showed him was a start.

IT TOOK GUS THIRTY MINUTES TO find the car Zeno had told him about. New tires saved the old cruiser from sliding off the road. The tires cost more than the car was worth. Abe Briggs, Gus's uncle and the county attorney, had grumbled that Gus should have paid for the tires himself, not the county, since the cruiser, almost twenty years old, was not an official vehicle anymore but Gus's private property, purchased from the county for fifty dollars. A new cruiser was on order.

The gray Dodge was nose down in the weeds. Not much damage. The driver hadn't been going fast. Dodges were popular in the county, but Gus thought this one belonged to Heidi Newsome. She was a widow and didn't farm anymore. She leased her fields to a neighbor who planted corn and tobacco. But she grew pumpkins and set them out on a table by the roadside for anyone to take.

Gus shouldered aside the prickly branch of a holly tree, eased open the passenger door, and found the registration in the glove compartment, in an envelope with four years of them. Mr. Newsome had bought the car new in December '55. The farm was two miles away. Gus wondered if Mrs. Newsome had walked home.

A shock of corn leaned by the porch steps. A Christmas wreath hung on the front door. Gus knocked. Inside, a dog barked. Mrs. Newsome opened the door, holding onto the dog, a shepherd mix, by its collar. She commanded the dog to sit and hush its barking.

"Found your vehicle," Gus said.

She looked at Gus. "Didn't know I lost it."

"I meant I noticed your Dodge in the weeds."

She wore a wool hat. Her brown eyes matched her sweater, which was coming apart and showed a pink one under it. Her jeans were tucked into rubber boots. "I phoned Buster's towing. He's real busy."

"How'd you get home?"

"The man who picks up milk and drives it to the dairy gave me a ride. I could have walked though. My old bones haven't quit me yet." She petted the dog. "Right, Sparky?"

The dog kept its eyes on Gus. "Forgot my purse."

"Didn't see it."

"Might have slid off the seat."

"I'll look on my way back to the office."

"Let me know. I had thirty dollars cash. Just bought the purse. A Christmas present to myself."

"You were out early, weren't you?"

"Since Miss Bright has the flu, I'm doing some baking for the diner. Delivered two dozen biscuits. The money was what Mr. Bowen owned me."

"Your car didn't appear damaged. You'll be on the road again. Be careful. Snow's in the forecast. Maybe tomorrow."

"Maybe today. I can smell it."

What Gus could smell was the whiff of kerosene from a space heater that clung to her clothes. "Hope you're wrong," he said.

"Sheriff, snow's a beautiful happening. Sparkles the stubble, glistens our fallow fields."

"Changes the roads for sure."

"You need to free your mind from your job, Sheriff. See the world differently." She pointed to the sky. "Gray isn't it."

"Yes, ma'am."

"Look closer. It's not one unrelieved horizon. There's a variety of tones in it, subtle differences."

"I'm not seeing too well these days."

"That woman, that Blossom Hall, she sees fine. Lovely passages in her writing describing our fields and skies. But I needn't tell you. I'm sure you read her work. Shame if you haven't. She dedicated it to you."

Gus nodded and reached out to pet the dog. It growled. Gus pulled back.

"Nothing personal, Sheriff. Takes a while for Sparky to trust you."

"I'll check on your purse," Gus said and stepped away from the door.

While he was searching the Dodge, Buster Green arrived and backed into position to winch the car out of the weeds. He climbed down from the cab and pulled the fur collar of his bomber jacket higher around his neck. "Making good money today," he said. "Fifth job so far. Got five more."

"If it snows, you'll be a rich man," Gus said.

"No," Buster said. "Folks can see snow and they stay home until it melts. They don't see ice, so they don't think it's there and they get in trouble." Buster pushed his hands into thick gloves. "Just the opposite of religion—folks not seeing something and believing in it." He chuckled while he dragged a chain from his truck.

"Tell Mrs. Newsome I didn't see her purse," Gus said.

—⁓—

TRAVIS HAD REHEATED THE LEFTOVER COFFEE. "Bitter," he said when Gus asked him how it tasted. "Soon as I finish I'll go patrol."

"Stop by Persons and the Wilburs, make sure they have enough firewood to keep warm."

"What if they don't?"

"We'll find them some."

"Sheriff …" Travis put his cup aside.

"What were you going to say?"

"When I'm sheriff, I won't know the county like you do."

"You'll learn it."

"I'm referring to the people."

"You'll learn them too."

Travis lifted his jacket from the coat tree by the hall. "I've been meaning to ask, what's Miss Blossom doing? You haven't mentioned her lately."

"She's spending the holidays in Mexico."

"Mexico?"

"With a friend."

"What kind of friend?"

"Male."

"She write you?"

Gus assumed their joining up, as Blossom called it, the time the autumn before when she had returned to Harr County and spent the night in his bed, satisfied the long yearning she had for him because her letters had become more about her career than her feelings and what their future together might be. "A card at Christmas," Gus said.

"The male have a name?"

"Chip something."

Travis zipped up his jacket. "Chip Parks?"

"Sounds right."

"He's kind of famous, isn't he?"

"For what?"

"Being handsome and being a movie star, the next James Dean."

"Check on the Reynolds. They live in the cabin on the Darwin farm. Mr. Reynolds hasn't been well lately."

"See, I wouldn't know something like that, who's sickly and all, but you do."

"Only because Zeno doctors the county and tells me what he thinks I ought to know."

"I know I ought to know more than I do," Travis said and

disappeared down the hall. The door opened and closed. A cold draft rustled the posters on the corkboard.

Gus spent the rest of the morning catching up on paperwork.

When Travis returned, he informed Gus that everyone he had checked on was warm and cozy but not happy. Harr County might get four or five inches of snow. Travis asked Gus to have the diner send over a sandwich—grilled cheese with bacon on it, and a pickle.

The diner was nearly empty. "I'm not fond on winter," Wally Bowen said.

Gus looked up from his menu. "I spoke with Mrs. Newsome this morning, and she reminded me that the season can be beautiful. We need to look for it."

"I spoke with her too. She reminded me I owed her money."

"Driving home, she slid off the road. Now her purse is missing and the money."

"Is that why you're here?"

"Wally, I'm here because it's noon and I'm hungry."

"Not the usual noon. Only you and three others in the whole place."

Gus recognized Mr. and Mrs. Jensen but not the older man sitting by himself at a corner table.

Wally leaned over the counter and whispered. "Never seen him. His Chevy is parked by the Jensens' pickup."

Gus nodded, glanced at the menu again, and ordered the pot roast, something hot and filling. He wouldn't get much supper unless he shopped at Spaid's store on his way home and bought groceries. With snow predicted, most everything would be sold out.

Wally wrote Gus's order on his pad and disappeared into the kitchen. A minute later he came back. "Shorthanded today," he said. "Penny Bright's about over her flu, but Marla caught it. Just me and the cook."

Gus said, "Travis is going to be disappointed. Marla usually brings him his sandwich."

"I'll have to send it with you," Wally said and headed for the kitchen again.

Gus missed Marla. She was shy and sweet, always smiling for the customers. When he told her who shot her father, she apologized for his causing Gus so much trouble.

Wally brought Gus's lunch and sent Travis's order to the kitchen. The man in the corner finished his meal. While Wally rang up his bill, the man selected a toothpick from the cup by the cash register and studied Gus while he cleaned his teeth.

"You the sheriff?" the man asked.

Gus turned around. "Yes, Sheriff Salt."

"Have something for you," the man said. He left and returned with a handbag, which he set on the counter. "Found it this morning on the road. Thought it was a dead animal at first. My eyes aren't very good, and the light was bad that time of day."

"Ruffin Road?" Gus asked.

"Believe so. I'm just visiting.'"

"Were you coming or going?"

"Going."

"From?"

"Sheriff, I paid a call on a local lady who gave me shelter when I was in no condition to drive."

Gus smiled at Wally. The man was about sixty. His overcoat was worn but expensive. Polo coat Gus thought it was called. The man's hat was city, but his trousers and boots were country. His hands were rough and chapped, and he needed a shave. The way one side of his coat sagged, Gus wondered if the man had a bottle in his pocket.

"I noticed a car off the road too," the man said. "About a mile away."

The handbag's brown leather was scuffed from the pavement. Otherwise the bag looked new. A comb and a handkerchief inside. No money.

"It's like I found it," the man said.

"Did you think about giving it to your local lady?"

"Crossed my mind, but I don't keep what doesn't belong to me."

"I appreciate that," Gus said. "What's in your pocket, is that something your local lady gave you?'

The man glanced at Wally, then back at Gus. "Forgot I had it," the man said. "It's not opened. You want to see?"

"Don't need to," Gus said, "but I advise not opening it until you're where you're going."

"Enjoyed my meal," the man said and started for the door.

"If you visit Miss Strother again, give her my regards," Gus said. The man stopped, turned, and stared. "I know when her husband's away she needs company."

Wally didn't laugh until the man was gone, then he wrapped Travis's sandwich and placed it, some chips, and a pickle in a bag for Gus to carry to the office. "What's Strother's sentence this time?"

"Five years. He'll serve three."

"You sorry what happened?"

"I kept warning him, but with the amount of liquor he was selling, the feds weren't going to be easy like I was being."

"Don't you imagine Miss Strother might welcome three years off from her husband?"

"She does favor variety."

"The spice of life?"

"She probably thinks of it that way."

The air outside felt wet and cold. At least the hazy sun had melted the ice. Gus handed Travis his lunch, explaining that Marla was out with the flu.

"There's a crowd at Spaid's stocking up on provisions," Travis said. "Folks thinking snow before evening now."

"After you eat, you better walk over there and direct traffic if you need to. Zeno saw the Hunt brothers throw something off the Harr bridge. After I take Mrs. Newsome her bag, I'm going to see if whatever the Hunts got rid of floated away or landed in the weeds."

———

THE WOOD STOVE KEPT THE COTTAGE WARM. The nearby shed that Tony Crim had converted into his studio was too cold for him to paint, an excuse to spend his afternoon with Neva. They had drunk a bottle of wine with lunch, a French lunch he called it— fruit, crusty bread, and cheese. Definitely not French without the wine. Afterwards they lay in Tony's narrow bed, which rattled and squeaked as they enjoyed each other.

"This cottage reminds me of the little house where my father died," Tony said, "except there were no fields outside. It was behind a tall house in Montmartre. There was a lovely garden, which made it very private. His mistress found him collapsed near the koi pond. He died in her arms."

"Don't die on me," Neva said.

"If I did, I would die happy, like my father."

"What about your mother?"

"She was French. She understood."

"You inherited the gallery?"

"Yes, maman wasn't interested in art, although we had some fine paintings at our house."

"How old were you?"

"That was January 1940. I was twenty-four. We all knew what was going to happen. Before the Nazis arrived, maman moved to her sister's in Brittany and caught pneumonia. She died in May. After the Germans arrived, I was naïve enough to think that because I wasn't a Jew or French I could leave when I pleased, but the Germans were difficult."

Tony remembered the way one of the officers had smirked as he studied Tony's documents. Sylvester Crim, Tony's father, had become a French citizen, but Tony had been born in Philadelphia and held an American passport, which the officer, instead of handing back to Tony, tossed on top of a pile of other passports that the officer was keeping for further consideration.

"And greedy," Tony said. "I practically had to give the gallery away."

"I'm glad you made it here," Neva said.

"I didn't know the South could be so cold."

Neva guided his hand down her body. "We know how to keep warm."

Tony raised her hand and kissed it. She watched him walk across the room to add more wood to the stove. He was tall and slender, his face tanned even in winter from all the hours he spent outdoors. His eyes were gray. Staring into the distance, he tended to squint. He combed his hair straight back. She had asked if he ever painted himself. He preferred not to paint men, he answered. One afternoon a month earlier, when the weather had been unseasonably warm, she had undressed, and he had sketched her sitting on a chair under the apple tree behind the cottage, her pose languid and provocative, her legs apart. Later he had knelt and kissed her there.

Tony returned to bed. "Who was the first girl you fell in love with?" Neva asked.

Neva lay on her side, Tony behind her. He stroked her hips and she reached back to touch him.

"Marie," he said. "Marie Kessler."

"You were how old?"

"I was twenty-two. She was sixteen and very rich."

"You weren't very poor."

"You don't get as rich as the Kesslers in the art business. Also, she was Jewish. I wasn't."

"You're saying your love was unrequited?"

"We never met."

"I don't understand."

"I fell in love with her portrait. There were two, the one Otto Kessler, her father, commissioned and brought to the gallery for my father to see and the one the painter did from memory. Kessler didn't know about it. The painter was giving me lessons, otherwise I wouldn't have seen it either."

Tony shifted his hips, bending his body from Neva's hand. "The painter's name was Shüle. In the official portrait she's seated primly in a chair in front of a window, the light glowing in her black hair. Her purple dress is formal, fashionable, and appropriate. Her necklace is a family treasure. The emeralds match her eyes and the cat's, some sort of Russian breed, a family pet, sitting on her lap. In the other one, she contemplates her nakedness reflected in a long mirror. Her beauty was overwhelming, haunting. Shüle's detail was exquisite. He was very good with skin."

"What happened to Shüle?"

"He was German and assumed when they took over they would leave him alone. They didn't. They expected him to give them information about the French. Instead he gave the Resistance information about the Germans. They figured it out and shot him."

"What about the portraits?"

"Otto sent the one he knew about to Geneva, private storage he had there managed by one of the banks. He didn't want a single German to see it or even breathe on it." Tony lay on his back now, his arm across his face, hiding his eyes. "Shüle destroyed the other one before it destroyed him. He could paint her, but he couldn't have her."

"Did the Kesslers survive?"

"Marie's mother left France in March. Otto had purchased a flat for her in London. He wouldn't leave his art behind. Marie decided to take her chances. In June the Germans marched into Paris. It didn't take them long to find their way to Kessler's estate in Le Vésinet. A deal was struck. The Germans got the mansion and Kessler's art. He and Marie got their freedom. At least that's what I heard." Tony moved his arm and stared up at the ceiling. "Le Vèsinet was charming then."

———

Sparky whined behind the door while Mrs. Newsome stood on the porch, examining the handbag.

"It's mine," she said, wiping her palm across the leather. "Doesn't appear run over or anything." She opened it and peered inside. "My money?"

"No money," Gus said. "Just a comb and a handkerchief. No lipstick, stuff like that."

"I'm too old and ugly for lipstick or cosmetics. What about a change purse and my billfold?"

"Gone."

"My license too, and my charm."

"What's that?"

"A four-leaf clover in a piece of plastic on a key chain. Souvenir from the state fair. Not worth anything. Paid a quarter for it and that was too much." Mrs. Newsome wiped the bag against her jeans. "I used to have a Lucky Lindy medal, but I gave it away." She spread her fingers. "About as big as a silver dollar. Lindbergh on one side, his plane on the other. You need me to come to the station and write all this down, make it official?"

"Can if you want to."

"Meaning it won't matter one way or the other?"

"I don't think we're going to find thirty dollars and identify it as yours. Your name's on the license. If we find it, you'll get it back. I'll keep in mind your change purse, your billfold, and your clover. If we find any of those, we'll bring them by."

Gus tipped his hat and was about to leave. He noticed a tractor driving across the field toward the barn behind the house. "Mr. Ross," Mrs. Newsome said. "He farms my land."

"His is the next farm over, isn't it?"

"His and the Fisk place. Ross's girl helps me in the house some. Not seen her now a week or so. Probably down with the flu. Haven't seen the painter either. Too cold for him."

"I thought the Ross girl moved to Charlotte."

"You mean Nancy, the daughter. She did move. I mean the girl who boards with the Rosses. She's not a girl really.

Must be on the bright side of forty or the dark side of thirty. Somewhere in there. Used to stay in Kingsville. Mute. Can't utter a word. Smart, I think, but choicy about communicating with anyone. Carries a pad of notepaper with her. Doesn't use it much. I'm not surprised you don't know about her. She's the person I gave the Lucky Lindy to."

"Tell me about the painter."

"Tony something. From up north. Introduced himself late August, when the tobacco harvest was done. A bit late this year. Asked if I'd mind if he walked the farm and painted. I answered my barn could use a coat. He laughed and said he only painted pictures. I told him to keep away from the hog pen. It's way behind the barn. You can't see it from here. The boar gets loose sometimes. Otherwise he could go where he wanted. Won't matter next time he comes. The hogs are gone and I didn't get to enjoy one ham or jowl. I had to shoot 'em and let 'em lay, vet's orders. He said to burn everything. Did the killing this morning, right after you left. Do the burning tomorrow. I don't have the heart to face it today. Dry as it's been, I feared starting a fire until that rain we had before this cold spell set in."

"What was wrong with the pigs?"

"Some unpronounceable disease thanks to a sow I imported from King County."

Gus said, "You've had some back luck lately. Not sure your charm did you any good."

"I'd still like it back."

—⁓—

THE BRIDGE OVER THE RIVER BETWEEN Harr County and King County had recently been named the Jessup Bridge in honor of William Jessup, who had flown missions in World War II and the Korean conflict and become a celebrated test pilot before perishing in a crash the previous winter. But most people still called the bridge the Harr Bridge since it went over the Harr River.

Gus parked his cruiser in the dirt area on the Harr County side and scuttled down the bank. Frost had flattened the weeds and curled the leaves with ice. The river was running low. Gus pushed his way through the cattails. The usual trash, mostly bottles and cans from the restaurant and picnic tables upstream. Whatever the Hunt brothers had thrown off the bridge had probably floated away. Cold as it was, Gus wasn't eager to keep looking.

He climbed back to the car and tried to coax some warmth from the heater. By the time he reached Levoy, the first flakes were floating over the town. He didn't recognize the faded green DeSoto parked in front of the station.

Travis said, "Here's the sheriff," and the man seated in the chair by the table with the coffeepot stood up."

"Donald Hastings," the man said and held out his hand.

Gus scanned the man's black clothes and white collar. "Father Hastings?"

"You can call me that, or Donald, or Don. Never cared for Donny. I've been assigned to resume services at the chapel on Chapel Road."

"Pleased you're here," Gus said.

"Travis has been filling me in, how Father Pierce's widow has returned to the community and married Mr. Levoy."

"The chapel has been closed for a while. The congregation

has probably dwindled," Gus said.

"I understand it was never robust to begin with."

"True."

"And yourself, were you a parishioner, Sheriff?"

"I wasn't.

"Though I've been told from time to time your vehicle has been seen parked in front of the chapel."

"From time to time I check to make sure there's been no harm or mischief. The county has its share of troublemakers, like anyplace else."

"But you linger."

"Sometimes."

"To enjoy the peace?"

"You could say that."

Travis was seated at his desk again, filling out a form, pretending no interest in the conversation while listening carefully. Gus's private life appeared routine and predictable, but Travis suspected there was more to Gus than met the eye: a solitary figure without the comfort of female companionship or even needing any; a competent rural sheriff who bent the law some to give people the benefit of the doubt; a man with few enemies and no close friends other than Percy Levoy, who was old enough to be Gus's grandfather. Yes, there was Blossom Hall and the suspicion Gus had given in to her wishes on one occasion the previous year when she had returned from California to attended Percy's wedding to Ruth Pierce, her excuse to ask Gus for a place to stay the night before she departed for California the following day. Recently, however, Blossom was photographed holding hands with a handsome young actor at a luxury hotel by the Pacific Ocean. Perhaps that was publicity and meant nothing. So much of the world Travis didn't understand.

Father Hastings and Gus had stopped talking and were studying each other. Gus wasn't the one smiling.

"I'll take my leave then," Father Hastings said.

The door opened and closed. The wanted posters fluttered and went still. The sky was filled with snow now.

Travis stood at the window and looked out. "'Arrives the snow,'" he said. "'The …,'" he hesitated, "'the whited air hides hills and woods.' Don't recall the rest."

Now Gus smiled. "Who wrote that?"

Travis pointed to the poetry book on his desk. "Mr. Emerson."

—◦∿◦—

AT FIVE THE NEXT MORNING Gus heard the county plow clearing his snowy lane. At six the radio reported an accumulation of four inches. Current temperature twenty-eight headed toward an afternoon high of thirty-eight, enough to melt most of what had fallen, but morning driving would be difficult.

Gus washed his cereal bowl and coffee cup, made his bed, and brushed his teeth. He used the broom from the kitchen to sweep the snow off his cruiser. He found the scraper under the front seat and cleared the windshield. The stars were out. The world, what Gus could see of it, was still and white and silent.

Gus followed where the plow had cleared one side of the road from the county garage to his cottage, flashing his lights to warn drivers that the cruiser was in the wrong lane, but no cars were out. The other cruiser, the one the deputies used, was parked in front of the station, about an inch of snow on the hood. Probably another inch had melted after Duncan Speed, the night deputy, had given up patrolling.

Duncan was sitting at the deputies' desk. "I didn't want to go into a ditch, so I knocked off early," he said. "Coffee's still warm if you want it."

"Maybe later. Any problems last night?"

"No problems. We have a guest though, a hitchhiker wanting a ride to Kingsville. I told her no one was out driving, and she was welcome to sleep in a cell if she cared to. Better than freezing to death. She agreed."

"Got a name?"

"Brenda Smith."

"*Smith*, you sure?"

"I took her at her word."

"I'll wake her," Gus said.

Gus walked past three empty cells and through the washroom that separated the male and female prisoners.

The cell door was open, the woman curled under the blanket Duncan had given her.

"Miss Smith?"

The woman brushed her hair away from her eyes. Gus watched as she loosened the blanket and sat up. Her shirt was too thin for winter, so was her skirt, which she pushed down to cover her knees. Gus picked up the blue jacket on the floor. The cuffs were frayed, and the denim gave off an acrid tobacco smell.

Gus handed her the jacket. "Brenda Smith, that's your name?" She nodded and reached into the jacket pocket. Instead of identification, she fished out a crumpled package of cigarettes.

"Match?" she asked.

Gus shook his head. "Hungry?"

"Need to pee," she said.

"I'll be in the office," Gus said.

A few minutes later she reappeared, wearing the jacket and a pair of boots that Gus had seen in the corner of the cell. At least her feet would be warm. She thanked Duncan for giving her a place to sleep. Gus pointed to a chair and offered her a donut and coffee. The diner wasn't open yet.

Lately her morning stomach was queasy, she said. She held the mug in both hands and sipped the coffee, then nibbled the donut before she pushed it away. She was spare and pale, her hair long and lank. Gus didn't think blond was its natural color.

"According to my deputy, you were headed to Kingsville."

"I live there," she said.

"Do you work there too?"

"Yes." She had the cigarettes in her hand again.

"What kind of work?"

"Miss Jean's Salon."

Duncan was searching his desk for a match. "Hairdresser?" Gus asked.

"Shampoo girl, and I sweep up."

Duncan shut the drawer. "Sorry," he said.

Gus continued, "Last night, were you visiting someone? Someone who might give you a ride home?"

She shrugged and said, "My boyfriend quit me. Wouldn't even open the door."

"But he lives here?"

"Some of the time."

"Would you tell me his name?"

"He wouldn't like it. He's mean."

"I'm not going to tell him.'

"He'd find out."

"Okay, suit yourself. Do you have any money?"

"You asking if I'm a vagrant so you can arrest me?"

"No, I'm asking because I don't want to send a woman dressed for summer out on a winter morning without having money to buy a meal or pay for a ride."

"You know someone who would take me?"

Gus glanced at Duncan. "My Jeep will carry you," he said. "No charge."

"Show me the money you have," Gus said. "I want to be sure."

She reached into her pocket, took out her cigarettes, and reached in again. "Seventeen dollars," she said, showing Gus a crumpled ten, a five, and two ones. She bent down quickly and picked up the card that fell out when she unfolded the bills.

"You're on your way then," Gus said.

———

"Passed Duncan on the highway," Travis said. He unzipped his jacket and hung it up. "Going to King County. He won't find much open."

"We had a guest who needed a ride to Kingsville. She calls herself Brenda Smith. I'd say she's twenty years old, maybe a year or two more. Except for a denim jacket, she was dressed for summer and had seventeen dollars and no identification that I'm aware of or she cared to show me. She dropped an appointment card. Looked like one from Wooten's clinic."

"You going to ask him?"

"I'll patrol and stop by the clinic if I have a chance."

"You won't find the roads like you want them."

"They never are," Gus said.

Travis stood at the window and watched Gus drive away. Then Travis surveyed the office, everything is its place. Anytime anyone moved a chair, Gus moved it back. He kept everything on his desk just where he wanted it to be. The thing about the roads: he would like them clean and dry, no trash, no litter, no signs tipped or bent, and no cars, no people. Only a perfect, placid emptiness.

Travis settled into his chair, put his feet up on his desk, and took the new book Miss Tolley at the library had given him: *Thirty Days to a More Powerful Vocabulary*. There was probably a word or two in it that Gus didn't know. It surprised Travis how many he didn't know and had never heard anyone use before.

—⟨∿∿⟩—

THE NOOK WAS THE ONLY RESTAURANT in Ruffin. Gus sat at the counter and ordered a bowl of chili with extra crackers. He was almost finished when Zeno sat down beside him.

"You lost?" Zeno asked.

"And now I'm found?'

"Don't think so, Sheriff."

"Nice hymn though. You agree?"

"I do." Zeno unbuttoned his jacket. "This poetry group Miss Tolley's got going one night a week, I know Travis attends. You know who else?"

"Not sure."

"I heard the man who bought the field on Girty Road from Percy goes. What's his name, Rubin something, the fellow Piney Nix dislikes so much?"

"Rubin Dazzle."

"What does he do?"

"He's planning to develop some sort of project."

"Perhaps a community of trailers like the one he's living in, housing for the less fortunate, though I don't believe Mr. Dazzle counts himself among them."

"I think he has some resources."

"Speaks five or six languages, I'm told. Lived all over."

"Would you object to trailers?"

"Not really. Chili any good?"

"Excellent."

Zeno waved to the waitress and ordered. "Mr. Crim, Neva's lover, only speaks three languages—French, German, and English. Unless the language of love counts," he added sarcastically.

Gus opened another package of crackers. "We let a young woman sleep in the jail last night. She said her name is Brenda Smith. I think she has an appointment at the clinic."

"And what has she to do with Mr. Crim?"

"Probably nothing. Why?"

"Transitions, Sheriff. You lack them. We were talking about one thing and you jumped to another as if my topic is less important than yours."

"Finish what you were going to say."

"I have. Carry on."

"Do you know a Brenda Smith?"

"*Know* is a loaded word."

"I'll rephrase. Does the clinic have a patient named Brenda Smith?"

"No."

The waitress set down Zeno's lunch and refilled his water

glass. "Let me describe her," Gus said. "Twenty or twenty-one, dyed blond hair, gaunt, pale—"

"Brenda Call," Zeno said. He savored his chili. "I agree. It's excellent."

Gus said, "Tell me about her."

Zeno sighed. "You know how I feel about privacy."

"Last night we found her on the highway. She wasn't dressed for being there. I'm concerned about her."

"You want to know what's going on."

"Yes."

"Tell me what you think is happening."

"I'm not sure why she was over here seeing you. There are doctors in King County."

"That makes you suspicious?"

"Yes."

"What else?"

"She said she worked at Jean's Salon, which is on Long Street near the Railroad Hotel."

"You are correct."

"The hotel provides female company for its visitors."

Zeno smiled. "Ergo Miss Call is a call girl?"

"Perhaps."

"Ah, I'm pleased there's hesitation in your accusation." Zeno set down his spoon and snapped his fingers. "Hesitation is your accusation—got a nice rhythm. Reminds me of something Danny Kaye would sing in one of his movies." Zeno stared up at the ceiling. "I wonder if Blossom has met him."

Gus finished his chili and asked for his check. "Miss Call said she had a boyfriend in Harr County."

"If you get a name, pass it on."

"Any reason?"

"She's going to add weight soon."

Gus nodded. "I thought she might be pregnant."

"I prefer to say she is with child. Suggests blessing and expectation, not demand and necessity."

The waitress laid Gus's check on the counter and started to walk away. Zeno said, "Bonnie, have you met the sheriff?" She shook her head. "Let me introduce you. Bonnie L.—Sheriff Salt. Sheriff Salt—Bonnie L." She reached across the counter and shook Gus's hand.

Zeno picked up the check. "My treat."

Gus thanked Zeno and nodded to Bonnie. The sun had warmed the cruiser. Gus sat and waited for Zeno to come out. When he did, Gus rolled down his window. "Tell me about Bonnie L.," Gus said.

"She's not my two other Bonnies—Bonnie B. and Bonnie M. Bonnie L. is one of my projects."

"A young woman you're helping, like Miss Call?"

"They need help, one way or another. The docs in King County are too prissy to treat folks who can't pay. They call that being professional."

"Is Bonnie pregnant?"

"Not anymore."

"Does she know Miss Call?"

"She recommended Brenda seek my services."

"Same as Bonnie's?"

"I'm providing prenatal care. I'm not sure what her plans are after the baby is born."

"Did you arrange for Bonnie to work here?"

"I did, but I'm not sure how that will turn out either. I hope for the best. Any more questions?"

"Not for you," Gus said. He watched Zeno drive away.

"Still hungry?" Bonnie asked when Gus sat down again. She was about the same age as Miss Call, only heavier and healthier.

"Your friend Miss Call—Brenda—do you know who her boyfriend is?"

"Roy."

"Roy Hunt?"

"That's the one. Brenda said they split up."

One must have a mind of winter
To regard the frost and the boughs
Of the pine-trees crusted with snow;

And have been cold a long time
To behold the junipers shagged with ice,
The spruces rough in the distant glitter

Of the January sun...

II

When Gus arrived on Thursday morning, Duncan had finished the night patrol and gone home. Travis was sitting at his desk, drinking coffee and reading.

"Sheriff, do you know anyone who suffers from triskaidekaphobia?"

"I'm not sure I know anyone who knows what it is."

"Fear of the number thirteen."

"Lots of people, I suppose."

"You have any phobias?"

"Name some."

Travis picked up his book. "Acrophobia, cynophobia, arachnophobia, ophidiophobia?"

"The first one—acrophobia. I don't like heights. Spiders and snakes don't bother me. What's cynophobia?"

"Fear of dogs."

"No, I like dogs. Cats too."

"You should get a pet. Keep you company after you retire."

Gus filled his coffee cup. "Is there a name for fear of advice?"

"If I learn it, I'll let you know," Travis said, shutting his book. "Think I'll go over to the diner and see if Miss Marla's back at work."

While Travis was zipping his jacket, the phone rang. "Wait," Gus said and asked the caller to repeat what she'd just told him.

Gus put down the phone and stood up. "A body," he said. "Newsome place. I need to phone Zeno. You can radio Tug from the cruiser."

Mrs. Newsome met them on the porch. Sparky whined and clawed at the door behind her. "I like dogs too," Travis said as they followed Mrs. Newsome.

"You wouldn't like this one," Gus said.

Most of the snow had melted from the fields except for tufts of white here and there. Mrs. Newsome explained about the disease and burning the hog pen the day before. Today she had gone out early to rake the embers. The wood was old and still wet from the rain days earlier. No sooner had she lifted the charred remains of roof piece when she saw the body.

"Jesus," Zeno said and turned away.

Mrs. Newsome stood back. Travis had brought the Polaroid from the office and took pictures.

"From what I saw in the war, a body will burn by itself for several hours," Zeno said.

"Are you making a general observation or does it have particular relevance to what we have here?"

"General observation. I could go into more detail.'

"As the county medical examiner, give me some detail about what's in front of us."

"Obviously the victim is burned to her bones, like the hogs. Skull is charred less than the rest. You'd expect that because there's less soft tissue. Teeth are present. You may get lucky and find a dental record for identification."

Gus hunkered down and studied the skull. He motioned

Zeno closer and pointed. "See what I see?"

"Fracture lines. We'll get a better look later."

The well pump worked. Miss Newsome filled a bucket and began to douse the few embers still smoking.

Tug and his son arrived and set to work. Travis watched. Zeno had patients to see. Gus walked Mrs. Newsome to her house.

Gus sat at the kitchen table while she made coffee. "I'd rather take some of my nerve medicine," she said, "but it's a mite early for that." She filled their cups.

The yellow walls needed painting, the green linoleum was wearing away, one of the cupboard doors sagged on its hinges and wouldn't close, but the east light filled the room. Sparky rested his head on his paws and stared up at Gus.

"I bet it's Betty, the Rosses' boarder," Mrs. Newsome said. "The one I told you about. She wandered."

"With anyone?"

"By herself. Like I said, she was mute. Not good company although …" Mrs. Newsome glanced around the room as if she needed something. Maybe her nerve medicine, Gus thought.

"Although what?"

"The Rosses heard rumors about her and men in town."

"In Levoy?"

"No, Kingsville. She stayed over there once, at the Johnson House, if you can believe that. Poor as she was, don't know how she could afford it, unless—well, men took a liking to her."

"Was she pretty?"

"Was once I imagine, but it's not necessarily pretty that men pay for."

"Anything else?"

"She liked flowers. Sometimes she'd go out in the fields and dig up a plant that I called a weed. She'd dig a hole in the garden, set it down, and call it a flower. Also, she liked to sew and make little things—towels and doilies. Some frilly, some useful."

"The other day you mentioned she carried a notepad. So she could write. Did she read much?"

"I saw her a few times holding the *Lantern*, but I couldn't be sure she was reading it. Could be the paper was a mystery she was contemplating, like we do God."

"Do you think we hold God in our hands?"

"Usually folks say it's the other way around, don't they?"

"They do."

"But your thought is interesting."

Sparky's eyes were closed now. "I'll speak to Mr. Ross," Gus said. "Hear what he has to say." Gus rose from his chair. Sparky's eyes opened.

"I suppose the *Lantern* will send someone out here."

"Probably."

"Sheriff, you could tell them they need to call ahead. I don't need disturbance."

"I'll try."

Sparky followed Gus to the hall, growling until Mrs. Newsome closed the door behind him.

Travis was standing by the cruiser talking to Clifford Ross, who had seen all the lights and vehicles and driven over to find out what was going on. He was short and thick, dressed in overalls and a flannel shirt. His sweater was unravelling at the elbows. Gus asked about his boarder.

Betty had been working in Kingsville at the Johnson House, doing washing and living in the basement. One day the previous spring she was riding her bicycle past the Rosses' house and saw Mrs. Ross standing at her mailbox. She was recovering from a broken foot and balancing on her crutches, trying to bend down for the letters she'd dropped. Betty picked up the letters and walked Mrs. Ross back to the house. She offered Betty a place to board if she'd stay for another month until Mrs. Ross's foot was healed. Betty accepted. She lived in a room behind the kitchen, a mudroom originally, framed into a space large enough to accommodate a bed, a table and chair, and a bureau. There was a separate area with a toilet and washstand. From time to time she visited with Mrs. Newsome and did some chores for her. They liked to garden together.

"Then one day Betty was gone. She left a note saying she missed the Johnson House." Mr. Ross shrugged. "But she came back. She settled into her old room like she'd never left."

"When was that?"

"September, right after Labor Day."

"Mrs. Newsome said she's disappeared again."

"After Christmas. The missus and I were concerned, but Betty was unpredictable. To tell the truth, Sheriff, another time or two she was AWOL. We were sure she spent the time with a man. She may be with someone now, safe and sound."

"I hope you're right.

"You'll want to see her room, won't you?"

"We will," Gus said.

"I'll ride you over," Mr. Ross said.

———∿∿∿———

THE ROOM WAS COLD, THE ELECTRIC HEATER TURNED OFF. "Betty didn't have much," Mrs. Ross said. "Wore pretty much the same clothes every day. Washed them though. She was mindful of good hygiene."

Mrs. Ross picked up the white hand towel on the table. "She was expert with needle and thread. She could make stuff and mend stuff real nice."

Mrs. Ross held out the towel for Gus to admire. On it Betty had sewn the figure of a man in blue overalls bent over planting a yellow flower by a green tree.

"What she carried with her I called a reticule. Clifford called it a green bag. Could have been silk. She must have sewn it together a few times much as she carried it."

"I don't see it."

"You wouldn't. She'd have it with her."

Gus looked in the washroom. Hand soap, toothpaste, and not much else.

"She was never sick or anything," Mrs. Ross said. "We took her to the dentist once. Doctor Burk in Kingsville. She needed a crown. I thought he'd fuss about a patient without a surname, but he said 'Betty' was good enough for him."

"Who paid?"

"Betty did."

"She had money?"

"Saved from her employment at the Johnson House, I imagine. The manager paid her in cash."

"Anything missing?"

Mrs. Ross glanced around the room again and straightened the towel on the table and shook her head.

"Poor thing, I miss her. I wasn't worried at first. Clifford probably mentioned that time to time she'd go off and fulfill her urges. I'm worried now though."

Mr. Ross was sitting outside on the kitchen steps, honing

a scythe. "Sort of reminds me of the grim reaper," Mrs. Ross said. "But better-looking."

Mr. Ross laughed and looked up at Gus. "Sheriff, marry a woman with a sense of humor. That's the best advice I can give you."

"Appreciate it," Gus said. "I suppose I'd better drive over to the Fisk place and ask them what they can tell me. George and Georgie, are those their names?"

"Right, but don't bother. No one's there. Only a couple of steers longing for company. I keep an eye on the place. Open the barn door in case the critters want to come in from the cold, but it don't seem to bother them."

"When are the Fisks expected home?"

"A few days, I reckon. A couple of new watering troughs showed up, so George and Georgie won't be far behind. Before the end of the month anyway. George plans to expand his herd."

"When did the troughs arrive?"

"I was there late Monday. They weren't. Went over early today, and there they were, all bright and shiny."

———

TONY SKETCHED AND TALKED.

"Tell me about the sheriff," he said.

Neva sat on the orange coverlet, her back against the wall. She wore black trousers that were too thin to wear outside in winter and a white shirt too sheer to wear anywhere expect in the privacy shared with a lover.

"He didn't plan on being a sheriff. He graduated from the university in Chapel Hill and was going to study writing with a professor at Harvard, but the war came along. The service wouldn't take him because his thyroid doesn't do what it's supposed to. When the only deputy the county had joined the navy, Gus's uncle, Abe Briggs, who's the country attorney, put Gus in the deputy's place. The old sheriff had his own health problems and retired. Gus became sheriff. That was 1943. He's been sheriff ever since."

"Someone mentioned you and he were close."

"One night I seduced him, a long time ago. He was young and tired and disappointed. His guard was down. We were close, if that's the right word, three times. Those minutes have provided the sheriff several years' worth of guilt." Neva laughed. "I guess now he's older and tired and disappointed."

"About what?"

"He doesn't think his past has amounted to much, and his future is murky, at best."

"You agree about his past?"

"He's been fair. He may have let some things go that he shouldn't, but people trust him, both blacks and whites. Harr County has been a peaceable place to live—not like next door."

"King County isn't peaceful?"

"So far, but the Negro population over there is restless. The sheriff is named Pope. That's what he thinks he is, someone the coloreds should kneel to and kiss his behind while he dispenses favors to his friends, who carry on various shady operations and slip Pope a share of the profits."

Tony laid down his pad and came over to Neva. He undid another button and lifted her shirt away from her breasts. "Three times, huh? Only three?"

"Only three."

Tony leaned down and tongued Neva's nipple. She inched

toward the wall. "Why don't you just lie beside me for a while." He did and she snuggled against him.

"Am I sharing you with your husband?"

"About a week ago he practically dragged me to bed. He hasn't done anything like that for a long time. He gets the sex he wants from Maggie, his nurse. That's been going on for years. Then there's the occasional dalliance at one of his out-of-town meetings. He doesn't lack for opportunity. The other night surprised me. I think he's jealous. You put a smile on my face. He wanted to find out if he could still do it."

"Did he?"

"You do it better."

"You sure?"

"Why don't you show me," Neva said.

———

GUS STOOD BY THE WINDOW IN Abe Briggs's office and watched the courthouse employees going home. The cold and snow had reduced the staff in most of the offices, including Abe's. Ora Green, his secretary, hadn't been at her desk since Monday.

Abe had filled his Jefferson mug with confiscated local whiskey and handed Gus the Washington mug filled with the legal kind. "Ora promised tomorrow. Her road's cleared now. She won't drive if there's even a flake of white stuff. Sort of ironic her brother's towing business must have made more than a few bucks off the white stuff. But"—Abe took a long sip—"my office hasn't had much activity since the holidays. However"—he sipped again—"your department is going to have your hands full with this body being found."

"I spent an hour with the *Lantern* reporter. Mrs. Newsome was angry, but she let him take some photos. She was about ready to sic the dog on him."

"What's the next step?"

"The state medical examiner's office is sending a man named Grogan to help."

"Help how?"

"First to confirm the skull was injured by a blow from something other than the roof falling on the victim, then consult with the dentist to identify whether the victim is the woman we think she is." Gus tasted his whiskey. "I need to see your county maps," he said.

Abe pointed to a deep row of filing drawers. A few minutes later Gus unfolded a detailed survey of the area that included the Newsome and Ross properties.

"What are you after?" Abe asked.

"Was the victim alive when he or she got to the hog lot, or was the victim carried there?"

Gus spread the survey on Abe's desk. "Where my finger is is where the pen was. On the north, the field borders Fisk property. See?" Abe nodded. "Now this squiggly line on the Fisk side is a lane big enough for tractors and equipment, at least that's the way I remember it. It's been awhile since I visited the property. I wanted to be sure I remembered right.'

"What's your point?"

"A person could drive a body there. It wouldn't be difficult to carry it the rest of the way across the Newsome's field to the hog pen." Gus stepped back and picked up his mug. "Or you could drive a person to the end of the lane, commit the murder, and take the corpse to the hog pen."

"Murder and all, aren't you getting ahead of yourself?"

Gus refolded the survey. "Way ahead."

"Travis said your other deputy took in a girl overnight."

"She wasn't dressed for the cold."

"According to my information, she wasn't much dressed at all."

"Your information is correct."

Abe raised his hand and stroked his bald head, the way he did in court when he was considering the meaning or veracity of testimony. "Gus, it worries me that some of the stuff in King County might wash our way. Did you wonder if that girl was servicing a customer over here?"

"She's one of Zeno's patients. She'd seen him and may have visited a boyfriend too."

"*Boyfriend*? Is that what customers are called now?"

"I think the term's accurate in this instance."

"Gus, understand my concern—Sheriff Pope lets the business in that hotel do what it does, but we don't need it over here." Abe thought a moment. "Some here may need it, but we're not going to have it. Keep an eye out. Be watchful."

"I always am."

"Perhaps, but you sure didn't go after Strother and some of his fellow shiners."

"I put Strother away twice. After the second time I decided to let the feds handle the situation."

"And you warned him."

"I *advised* the man what the consequences were. He chose to keep producing his product, and the feds chose to go after him for doing it."

Abe sighed. "I admit he made good stuff. What's in my mug isn't nearly up to his standards."

—⁓—

FRIDAY MORNING.

"Your old friend Roy Hunt is waiting in his cell to see you," Travis said. "Duncan brought him in last night. Sixty in a thirty zone. Intoxicated and quarrelsome."

"You mean drunk and disorderly?"

"Your uncle is always complaining my speech is limited. I'm trying to improve my diction."

"Think our prisoner's awake?

"I heard him yelling something."

Roy pushed off his blanket and sat up. "What's for breakfast, Sheriff?"

"The diner will send something over."

"When?"

"Soon as we finish talking."

"I'm already finished."

"Roy, it's Friday. I could keep you here until Monday, but you wouldn't like that."

"Neither would the ladies."

"They're what I'm here to talk about. Cooperate and I'll drop twenty off your sixty."

"What about the other stuff?"

"Convince me."

"Talking about ladies is my favorite subject, Sheriff. I had no idea it's something interested you."

"I keep some things to myself."

"You sure do. If I'd go as long as you without female companionship, I'd bust."

"Are you keeping company with anyone in particular?"

"No, sir, I play the field."

"You ever been with Brenda Call?"

"Once or twice. How do you know her?"

"We gave her shelter the other night. Was she coming from seeing you?"

"What other night?"

"Tuesday."

"The sixth. Old Christmas. No, sir, she wasn't seeing me."

"Do you visit some with Miss Harbaugh's ladies at the Railroad Hotel?"

"Like I said, Sheriff, I can't go too long or I bust."

"Is the hotel where you met Brenda?"

Roy folded the blanket and set it on his lap. "I might have," he said.

"You stay over there any, at the hotel?"

"A time or two."

"Must cost you something."

"I work. I'm employed. Money in my pocket. Brother Billy's always borrowing, not me."

"Where do you work?"

"Different places."

"Name one."

"When the weather's good, I help Piney Nix carpenter, rebuilding his station. You never did catch who burned it down, did you?"

"The man fled the county. We know who he is, but we can't find him."

"You'd think with local police, state police, and federal a man couldn't hide for long. Guess you're not all-powerful as you play at being."

"Guess not," Gus said. "Name another."

"Another what?"

"Another place you work."

"The hotel."

"Doing what? What are your duties?"

"'What are your duties.' You're beginning to sound like Doc Wooton, all stern and dignified."

"Have you spoken with the doctor lately?"

"A week or so ago."

"Feeling poorly?"

Roy smirked. "Needed to have my pecker checked."

"Everything all right?"

"It's going to be."

"An inconvenient infection?"

"Something like that. Doc's fixing me up."

"What about the hotel, what do you do there besides enjoying the ladies?"

"Run errands for Miss Harbaugh and her guests. And keep the peace sometimes."

"Errands? Like acquiring bottles of alcoholic refreshment when requested?"

"Things run different in King County. It's not like here."

"You mean you only need to walk over to the Crown Club, knock on the backdoor, and come away with what you need?"

"I know you've downed a drink there more than once."

"Roy, we're talking about you. Keeping the peace, is that how you got those scratches on your face and the bruises on your arms?"

"One of Miss Harbaugh's visitors was unruly," Roy said, "but I subdued him."

"What about your brother?" Gus asked. "Is he employed?"

"Billy works a couple of days a week at the Tuft's Feed and Implements in Bow, fixing equipment, but most farmers have their tractors and stuff put away until spring. He'll be full-time then." Roy spit on his palm and slicked it over his hair. "My stomach is growling, Sheriff. Most folks drink like I do, next morning the sight of food makes 'em puke. Not me."

"Go clean yourself up. I'll order something. Come to the office when you're ready."

"Two eggs, fried. Grits and a biscuit," Roy said.

A few minutes later Roy sat down in the chair Gus had placed in the corner by the coat tree.

"One other woman I'm interested in," Gus said. "She gets around on a bicycle. She's mute, doesn't speak. Some people call her Betty."

"Saw her last week."

"What day?"

"Thursday."

Gus and Travis exchanged glances. "Where?" Gus asked.

"Seen her walking over the Harr bridge, about seven o'clock in the morning. New Year's Day."

"Walking, not biking?"

"Pushing her bike."

"Alone?"

"Appeared that way."

"Seven. Are you usually on the road that early, especially first day of the year?"

"I don't like the hotel in the morning. It's all quiet, full of the smells of bodies and such."

Marla brought Roy's breakfast in a basket covered with a towel. "Use my desk," Travis said. She set out the meal. Travis put on his jacket to walk her back to the diner.

While Roy ate, Gus collected some paperwork. When Roy finished, Gus showed him where to write his name. "What am I signing up for?" Roy asked.

"What you've been charged with and that you'll appear in court next Wednesday morning." Gus handed Roy an envelope. "What you had in your pockets when Deputy Speed brought you in," Gus said. "Sign again if you agree we're returning everything."

Roy peeked inside the envelope, wrote his name, folded the envelope, and started to put it into his pocket.

"Dump it out," Gus said. He pointed to the desk. "Let me see what you have."

"My billfold and car key," Roy said. "And fifteen cents."

"Let me see."

Roy laid a dime and a nickel beside his plate.

"No, all of it. Everything," Gus said.

Roy shook the envelope over the desk.

"What's that on your key chain?" Gus asked.

"My good-luck piece," Roy said.

"A four-leaf clover?"

"Reckon so," Roy said.

"How's it working for you?"

"Except for my pecker, can't complain."

"My luck's been shifty lately," Gus said. "I'll swap you a dollar for your lucky piece."

Roy shrugged, undid the key chain, gave Gus the clover, and pocketed the dollar.

"Free to go?"

Gus handed Roy a slip of paper. "Your vehicle's at the county garage. Mr. Dent's running the place now. Give him the paper to claim your property."

"Kind of funny," Roy said, "a man named Dent working in a garage. Must be plenty of dents with all the trucks and school buses over there."

"The county has a sense of humor," Gus said. "But not where you're concerned. Keep out of trouble."

—∿—

MRS. NEWSOME HELD THE CLOVER UP TO THE LIGHT. "Sheriff, looks like mine." They stood on the porch again, Sparky by her side, eying Gus attentively.

"There must be dozens of them that look alike."

"Yes, but see this place here." She pointed to a gouge. "Sparky's tooth. I was sitting in the kitchen by the window watching the way the plastic around the clover reflected the light when Sparky grabbed it and I had to yank it out of his mouth."

"It's yours then," Gus said.

"The Lucky Lindy would be better. Sorry now I gave it away."

Gus started to leave and turned around. "Mrs. Ross mentioned that Betty always carried a little bag with her, a reticule she said."

"Betty did, except when she wandered outside. She'd leave it here."

"Did you ever open it?"

"Gracious, Sheriff, I wouldn't do that. I was curious, but I wouldn't examine what wasn't mine, something private and personal."

"Do you have any idea what she kept in it or a guess about the contents?"

"Pencils and a notebook for writing messages, I'm sure of that. Cap and scarf, she had those. I think she knitted both." Mrs. Newsome frowned. "And a bracelet she favored. Not

47

something expensive, just costume jewelry. Brown. Might have been wood or plastic. Never had a close look. Bakelite, maybe. I think that's what it was called. She wore it off and on. I sort of thought of it as her good-luck charm. Anyway, something that was important to her."

"How do you know that?"

"From the way she studied it and stroked it sometimes, like she was talking to it. Not her tongue, but her mind." Gus started to leave again and she paused. "When you going to hear, Sheriff—about identifying the body?"

"I'll have more information tomorrow morning."

"Tomorrow's Saturday."

"Somebody's lucky day," Gus said. He had a feeling it wasn't going to be his.

—◦◦◦—

TWO BLOCKS AWAY THE STEEPLE BELL of the Episcopal church was ringing four o'clock when Gus parked the cruiser near the Railroad Hotel.

Dark furniture filled the lobby. Some pieces were shabby; others, like the secretary desk in the corner near a spinet and a Martha Washington chair, were tasteful antiques. The carpet was worn through in places.

Gus had never been one of Miss Harbaugh's clients— guests, she referred to them—but he knew the routine, *protocol* in her words. If one only wanted lodging, one requested it at the desk, signed the register, and received a key to one of the rooms on the third floor. If one sought company, one told the room clerk he was there to meet a friend. The clerk then handed over a key and pointed to the stairs. One climbed to the second floor, opened a door with the key, stepped inside, let the door lock shut, gave the key to whomever asked for it, and was led into a room with a bar, music, and welcoming faces. Small, secluded rooms were available to anyone wishing to stay the hour or the night. Choose your partner and do-si-do, Travis said. Individual requests were always welcome.

The clerk stared at Gus and tried for a professional smile but managed a grimace instead. He uttered a stiff "Welcome to the historic Railroad Hotel."

"I'd like a word with Miss Harbaugh," Gus said. "Here, in the lobby," he added.

The clerk was about fifty, dressed in brown trousers, a striped Arrow shirt, and a clip-on bow tie. Gus couldn't see his shoes. Perhaps they were as brown as the clerk's eyes or black as his brows. "I'll phone up and see if she's available," he said, never taking his eyes off Gus while he reached for the house phone under the counter and asked for the missus. He looked away from Gus, slumped a little, thumbing the spine of the register while he waited. A woman's voice spoke and the clerk replied, "The sheriff, ma'am." The woman's muffled voice again, then another reply, "No, not him, the other one, Harr County." The clerk nodded. "I will," he said and hung up. "She'll be right down."

"Sheriff?" Gus stood admiring a watercolor hung on the wall by the desk. "The picture's new, I'm not. I'm old now." Miss Harbaugh reached out to shake Gus's hand.

Her gray hair was pinned back, her face was long and wrinkled. The blue of her eyes reminded Gus of winter sky reflected on a frozen pond. She wore a crewneck sweater, doeskin trousers, and silver sandals.

"May I offer you a beverage?" she asked. "Perhaps an herbal tea to restore the body?"

Gus declined. "Just need to ask about someone," he said.

"A woman, I imagine." Miss Harbaugh pointed to a faded settee. Seated, she asked, "What name?"

"Betty, but that may not be right. She's mute."

"Yes, I was first aware of her over a year ago, maybe longer. About the time that girl was kidnapped in your county, the one whose father was killed."

"Marla Slack," Gus said.

"Right, that girl. This Betty you're asking about worked at the Johnson House."

"Did she ever work for you?"

"Oh, Sheriff, no one *works* for me. I offer a living arrangement to five or six young women and teach them manners and the refinements of speech so that they are more presentable and employable. Others, knowing my generous nature, join me on weekends to take pleasure in companionship otherwise unavailable to them."

"Did Betty stay here, at the hotel?"

"She quit the Johnson House and showed up here one day."

"One day when, more or less?"

"Early June. My birthday's then. Won't say how old I am."

"What did she do?"

"Helped out with cleaning and laundry like she did at the Johnson House in exchange for meals and a place to lay her head. A storage closet suited her. There wasn't much I could teach her, being mute and all. Furthermore, she didn't take kindly to anyone telling her what to do. Sometimes I felt she thought she should be telling me what to do. We had a bit of a fracas here on Labor Day. Then she was gone."

"No one's seen her lately."

"Lay your cards on the table, Sheriff. News travels fast. Do you believe Betty is the body in the hog lot?"

"It's possible."

"Despite all those Quakers in your county, you've had your share of murders."

"Seems like it."

"I understand you're retiring."

"In April."

"Your deputy—Travis Pace—I see him every now and then." She laughed. "If he steps into your shoes, he'll need to step large, none of that petty pace stuff. You know, like the Bard said, 'Creeps in this petty pace from day to day.'" Gus stared at her. "We're not all semi-literate bumpkins, Sheriff."

She reached over and laid her hand on his knee. "And what about you? You going to author some stories, embark on that writing career postponed now how many years?"

Gus stood up. "I'm not sure what I'm going to do in April, but right now I need to speak to the manager at the Johnson House." He paused to admire the watercolor again: an abandoned house, slants of sun and shadows.

"The painter—some of my ladies posed for him."

"Crim, it that his name?"

"It is. Nice man. The ladies liked him." She smiled up at Gus. "They'd like you too."

"My skills with a paintbrush are minimal."

"I bet you've got some other skills, some you haven't used for a while."

"Enjoyed the conversation, Miss Harbaugh," Gus said.

Outside a raw wind blew across his face. He couldn't remember a January so cold. He walked the three blocks to the

Johnson House and asked to see Mr. Coombs, the manager.

"I know the girl you mean," he said. "She did housekeeping when needed, but she preferred doing laundry—most don't, hot machines and being in the basement all day. She even slept down there. Preferred a cot near the boiler, maybe because she couldn't speak. She didn't trust others, some didn't trust her. She spooked them."

"How long was she here?"

"Year and a half in all. So quiet you'd forget about her. She had a key for the basement. She could come and go like she was invisible. Then one day she vanished—"

"When?"

"Can't be specific, but the weather was turning, the forsythia was out. March, maybe. She liked to ride her bike, long rides in the country. Then about a month later she reappeared, just after Easter. She'd been living with a farm family."

"The Rosses."

"Yes, that's right."

"Then she quit you again?"

"I asked her to leave. The housekeepers didn't care for her. She made them uneasy, like she was always looking over their shoulders and judging them. She had an aura of being special. One of them complained she'd seduced her boyfriend. She'd offered herself to guests before. One gentleman returned to his room while she was changing his linen. He said she lifted the hem of her uniform, up to her thigh. It wasn't the first time. I suggested she might find accommodation at the Railroad Hotel."

"Do you recall when that was?"

"I can tell you exactly. June the second, a Monday. The high school was having a graduation dance here the next

Saturday, and I was concerned Betty might try to lure one of the young men astray. I paid her for the whole month." Mr. Coombs shrugged. "All these questions, Sheriff. You think she got burned up?"

"The remains haven't been identified."

"If it's her, she probably had the bag she carried all the time, and it probably got burned up too. She guarded it real careful, but once a couple of the housekeepers snatched it to see what was inside." Mr. Coombs stated to walk across the lobby.

"What was?"

"Nothing special, nothing much at all. No identification. Scraps of paper, pencils. Comb and a mirror, I think. She was kind of vain. She looked at herself a lot." Mr. Coombs rearranged a vase of bittersweet. "A warm hat, she had one of those."

"Money?"

"A few dollars."

"Did she wear jewelry of any kind? Watch? Ring?"

"Only a cheap plastic bracelet. She was fond of it."

Mr. Coombs continued across the lobby and stopped to straighten some magazines. "Can you remember anything else?"

"She never handed in the key I gave her, at least not to me."

Mr. Coombs turned a chair to face the fireplace. Two guests were seated watching the cheerful glow warming the room. Gus wondered at what temperature a body burned. Grogan could probably tell him, but he didn't really want to know.

Darkness was setting in. Crossing the river, Gus thought about the Hunt brothers throwing something off the bridge. Wind buffeted the car. Wasn't hard for Gus to talk himself out of searching the riverbank again.

—⁓—

SATURDAY MORNING. TRAVIS HAD THE DAY OFF.

Duncan signed out. "Oh, found this under the door. Guess someone left it last night." Duncan handed Gus an envelope. He waited until Duncan left to open it. The poem was typed on a sheet of white paper that looked torn from a tablet.

Where she has been?
Past Elm, past Spruce,
The golden goose,
Inquire within.

Gus thought about the poem while he checked the cells and brewed a pot of coffee. Elm and Spruce, streets Gus assumed. Levoy had neither. Kingsville had both.

He sat down with his coffee. He heard the door open. The wanted posters danced on the wall. Neva Wooton took off her gloves and unzipped her coat. She kept her coat on. She was dressed in a flannel shirt, jeans, and boots.

"Want coffee?" Gus asked.

"You make it too strong. Anyway, I'm not staying. More snow predicted, I need to shop before Spaid's sells out of everything."

"Crim, someone told me."

"Anthony Crim. Tony he's called," Neva said.

"I saw one of his paintings in the lobby of the Railroad Hotel."

"A couple of Miss Harbaugh's *ladies* posed for him."

"I remember you liked to be looked at," Gus said.

"I like to be *admired*. I recall you did some of that."

"I'm sure I did."

"Well, I didn't stop by to talk about what is and what was.

I saw a bicycle lying in the weeds on Girty Road near where the mysterious man who bought that field from Percy is living in a trailer. I thought you'd want to know. Not many people ride bikes around here. I recall seeing a young woman doing it before winter set in."

"The man's name is Rubin Dazzle," Gus said.

"What kind of name is that?"

"It's what an immigration agent wrote down when Mr. Dazzle got off the boat in New York. In Europe he was Dässel."

"Got off from where?"

"Cuba."

"Dazzle or whatever isn't Spanish."

"He was Austrian, living in France. For a price the Germans let him leave. One less Jew to deal with."

"Sounds exciting."

"He doesn't think of it that way."

"What's he want with Percy's field?"

"To be left alone."

"Then he's probably getting his wish. I've seen him in town occasionally, always by himself." Neva set her coffee cup aside. "Of course the same thing could be said about you."

"Guess so."

Neva stood up. "Gus"—she lifted her coat off the coat tree—"Gus, I wish I could provoke you into saying something, something with feeling." She zipped her coat and wrapped her scarf around her neck. "What do you hear from Blossom?"

"Nothing," Gus said.

"What do you hear *about* Blossom?"

"She's doing well."

"Getting her photograph in magazines, nuzzling up to some young leading-man type, standing on a beach somewhere, staring at the sunset. When dark comes, doing more than nuzzling, I imagine. What do you imagine?"

"I keep my thoughts to myself."

"So does Zeno, but I'm pleased to say Tony doesn't." Neva reached into her pocket and took out her gloves. "Honestly, Gus, if Zeno had said more and kept his manhood to himself— us—and not shared it with any woman who caught his fancy, I would have been faithful myself." She pushed her hands into her gloves. "But then I would have missed out on Tony."

Gus started to walk Neva to the door. The phone rang: Grogan from the state medical examiner's office. The posters fluttered and went still.

"Not who you thought it was," Grogan said. "No match with the dental records Doctor Burk gave me for a patient named Betty. She had a silver crown. The victim didn't. The temperature of burning wood wouldn't melt silver. Need to be twice as hot to do that."

Grogan explained that the skull had been fractured. The victim was probably dead before the fire. Difficult to believe anyone could survive such a blow. The bone damage was significant. Grogan recalled hogs being brained with a club hammer before they were butchered and asked if Gus had ever seen it. Gus said he had. He wished he hadn't. One blow never was enough.

Grogan hadn't told anyone else. "Let's keep this to ourselves," Gus said. "The reporter from the *Lantern* will ask. Tell him the forensic evidence is inconclusive."

Gus hung up and drove to Girty Road. He found the bicycle lying in the weeds in the deep swale near Rubin's mailbox. The handlebars were pitted with rust. Someone had repainted the fenders blue; their red reflectors were missing. He lifted the bike into the trunk of the cruiser.

Rubin Dazzle had paid a man to bulldoze and gravel a lane from the road to his trailer. Gus tooted his horn and parked the cruiser behind a Crosley, an unusual car in the county. Rubin opened the trailer door and waved Gus inside. Rubin pointed to the book open on the narrow table.

"I'm planning an orchard," he said, "deciding what trees. Will peaches thrive here?"

"With care," Gus said.

"Apples, of course. And pears, two or three varieties. What about plums?"

"I'd check with the state ag agent in Kingsville."

Gus apologized for interrupting and asked if Rubin had ever noticed anyone riding a bicycle nearby. Rubin thought a moment. "I haven't," he said. "Why do you ask?"

"I recovered a girl's bike near your mailbox."

Rubin remarked the weather had been keeping him inside lately. He wouldn't have seen a bicycle. He didn't expect mail, so he never looked for any.

Gus asked about the Crosley.

"The driver ran out of gas."

"In your lane?"

"He and a woman pushed it off the road. I told him he could leave it here."

"Did you know the man?"

"He was large and strong. He pushed and the woman steered. She left a note saying someone would tend to the vehicle soon."

"The man—black or white?"

"He was black, she was white, but I only saw her from a distance. I stayed inside. He said they didn't need my help."

Rubin returned to the topic of bicycles. "In Europe they were everywhere. I never see anyone riding them here. From time to time a couple of boys race motorbikes."

"Do they disturb you?"

Rubin shook his head. "Too cold for racing now."

"No one causing you trouble?"

"Someone came in the night."

"How do you know?"

"Footprints in the snow. I'm sure it wasn't the first time."

"Did the person do anything?"

Rubin pointed over Gus's shoulder. "The footprints stopped at the window."

The trailer was small enough that someone peering through the oval windows could see almost the whole inside.

"You keep the curtains drawn?"

"At night. But you can see shapes if you're looking in."

"Thicker curtains?"

"There's a person in Kingsville who might provide what I need."

"Do you spend much time there?"

"I enjoy the Johnson House. To my surprise the chef makes excellent sauerbraten and potato pancakes. His pork is wonderful."

"I'm concerned about a young woman who worked there. She rode a bicycle."

"*Die stumme*, the mute. Yes, I saw her."

"When was the last time?"

"Months ago."

"She's missing."

"I hope to no harm."

"I hope so too."

Gus leaned over the table and picked up the pad on which Rubin had jotted down the names of several kinds of apples. "May I have a piece? I need to write a note."

Rubin tore out a sheet and handed it to Gus. "Pencil?"

"Have one in the cruiser," Gus said.

———

SOME AFTERNOONS WHEN GUS HAD DRIVEN by the entrance to Twelve Trees, Percy Levoy had shut the gates. Gus had stared down the row of winter poplars at the porch and columns, a few wreathed with pine boughs, and seen smoke rising from the chimneys and decided not to intrude. Teddy, Percy's grandson, was having fits again and probably needed hospital care. The holidays always upset him. Ruth Pierce, now Ruth Levoy, saw Gus in town and said Teddy was a handful.

Now, though, the gates were open. Gus raised the brass ring and knocked. Mrs. Ravenel opened the door and smiled. "Sheriff Gus, how you been keeping?"

"Not liking winter much," Gus said.

Mrs. Ravenel closed the door, took Gus's jacket, and pointed down the hall. "Mr. Percy's with his books." She lowered her voice. "Miss Ruth's brooding somewhere."

"They're not getting along?"

"You know how it is, a May-December marriage. Miss Ruth feels cooped up. She needs a little sass."

"I'm not sure what you mean."

"I'm referring to activity of a physical kind."

"Like stretching one's legs, taking long walks?"

Mrs. Ravenel winked. "Legs are involved. Walking isn't. You understand?"

Gus squeezed her hand. "I do, but I don't think I'll offer Percy any advice on the matter. How is Teddy?"

"A bit calmer now. Got a new caretaker. Might be just the thing to put a smile on Miss Ruth's face, a bit of caretaking. Mr. Percy ain't doing his job."

"Like I said, I'm not going to offer advice, even if I had some to give."

"Mr. Gus, I observed you and Miss Blossom when she came back for the wedding. And I heard tell she left your house with a satisfied expression on her face. I believe you can handle yourself in the advice department."

"Perhaps, but I'd better stick to law enforcement."

"Stick to what?" Percy said. "I heard you mumbling out there in the hall. My ears still work."

Percy pushed back from his desk. Miss Ravenel added a log to the fire and gave Gus another wink as she left the room.

Percy was wearing brown loafers, brown corduroy trousers, and a brown wool shirt. He appeared tired. "I guess you have death on your mind," he said. "The *Lantern*'s reported a person burned up in Mrs. Newsome's hog lot."

"Died from a fracture skull, not the fire."

"Mrs. Newsome never welcomed strangers. She must have hated all the fuss."

"She couldn't do much about it."

"Suppose not. You staying long enough for a libation?"

"If you're offering."

Percy poured some whiskey into a tumbler and handed it to Gus, who held the glass up to the light, admiring the dark amber of the contents. Percy refreshed his own glass, then sat down at the table, Gus seated on the opposite side, a stack of books and maps between them.

"Ruth's after me to write a history of the county," Percy said.

"Sounds appropriate. Your family's been here as long as anyone's."

"I suspect she's trying to keep me occupied. A mind as old as mine requires activity or it fades away. At least that's the theory going around. Ruth's been reading up on aging. Some of the questions she asks me are too personal. She doesn't need to know the details of my urinations and such."

"I bet you enjoy her company though."

"She's not too cheerful lately. Winter's got her down, and it's hardly started."

"What about Teddy?"

"He's been a challenge, but I hired a new caretaker. Teddy took to her right away."

"Young woman?"

"In her thirties, I'd guess."

"Name?"

Percy hesitated. "Alice."

"Alice what?"

"Alice French. The other day Ruth found Teddy and Alice sitting on the floor looking at each other. Teddy was tracing her face with his fingertips. I joked maybe he was learning French. Ruth didn't think that was funny." Percy sipped his drink and contemplated the dance of flames in the fireplace. "When you're old, your sense of humor changes and you don't know it."

"You haven't lost yours yet," Gus said.

Percy put down his glass and faced Gus. "Blossom, have you lost her?"

"Percy, I never really had her, not in the way you mean, nothing permanent."

"I sure thought when she came here to say goodbye after spending the night at your place things between the two of you would last. Happiest I'd ever seen her."

"You've lived long enough to know better."

"And you haven't lived long enough to believe the opposite."

Gus's glass was empty now.

"Another?" Gus shook his head. "Come April, what are you planning to do with yourself?"

"The law school at Chapel Hill said they would consider my application."

"Have you sent for one?"

"Not yet, Percy, not yet." Gus stood up. "Tell Ruth I stopped by," he said.

"WHAT'S THE BUSINESS TONIGHT?" ROY ASKED.

Piney opened the window and flicked his cigarette into the night. Sparks flew up and disappeared. "Jew business."

"He don't go nowhere."

"That's because he got nowhere to go, not in Harr County. Jews are city people."

"I thought they lived in the desert."

"Used to, centuries ago. Hitler wanted to round 'em up and ship 'em back, let 'em do some more wandering, but it cost too much, so he decided to do something else."

"The gas chambers I heard about?"

"Don't believe everything you hear."

"You don't believe that's what Hitler did?"

"Not sure it matters one way or the other, not to me

anyway. But some folks want to make a stink. That war's over. Been another one since. Probably one coming. I'm concerned about the here and now, this Hebrew man in our midst."

"You planning to scare him into leaving?"

"First, I'm trying to understand why he bought Percy's land and what he's going to do with it. So we'll just park up the road awhile and see if any company comes to call."

"What about Deputy Speed?"

"It's nine o'clock. I know how he patrols. He won't be close for another hour. Sunday nights he don't come here at all."

Piney edged his Jeep off the road and parked. Roy lit a cigarette and took a pint of whiskey out of his jacket. "Go easy," Piney said and slunk down in his seat.

"Without the heater on an hour is about all I'm good for," Roy said.

"Must be nice and warm at Miss Harbaugh's, especially tonight."

"Saturday's are lively."

"You miss being there?"

"Not really. I'm not good at dealing with some of the Saturday customers, rough trade she calls 'em. That's why she hires one of Sheriff Pope's deputies to keep things peaceful. The weekday customers are kinda meek—orderly at least. Did have some fussing Labor Day."

"You ever consider asking visitors for money not to tell where they been?"

"If I did, Miss Harbaugh would have Pope himself teach me a lesson I don't want to learn. I like having all my teeth in my head."

Roy passed the bottle to Piney, who took a sip and made a face. "Where'd you get this?"

"A man told me ol' Strother stilled it before Sheriff Gus sent him away."

"The man lied," Piney said. "And Sheriff Gus was pretty much willing to let Strother do what he did. It was the feds who cracked down." Piney rubbed his chin and smiled. "You ever visit Strother's missis?"

"Me and Billy did a couple of times."

"Good times?"

"I enjoyed myself. Billy stayed in the car. He's shy."

"Shy what?"

"Not sure. We don't do stuff together much anymore. Billy stays mostly at home."

A fox emerged from the field, eyed the Jeep, and slunk across the road into the darkness.

"Who's the most unexpected person you ever saw at Miss Harbaugh's?"

"Mr. Dazzle."

Piney rubbed his chin again, harder this time. "You sure?"

"No mistake about it, but I'm not sure he was wanting pleasure. For a while there was a mute woman who washed and changed the linens. I think Dazzle wanted to tell her something. They went into a room together and closed the door. When they came out, they didn't appear to have done stuff."

"What about the woman?"

"I didn't much care for her. I tried to be friendly, but she always turned away. I could see she'd been pretty once. Her body still was, but her mouth was all twisted up. Vexed me how she ignored me, like I wasn't good enough for her, or something like that. I could have broke her neck and got away with it. A couple of times I come close. Got a tingle in my hands just thinking about squeezing her throat. Then one day she left and didn't come back. Even Miss Harbaugh didn't know where she'd gone. Sheriff Salt was asking about her. She might have burned up."

"I heard about that," Piney said.

Roy passed the bottle again. Piney took another swallow, scowled, and decided the night was too cold to stay out any longer.

———

GUS HAD FRIED A HAMBURGER and warmed some canned beans for supper. After he washed the dishes, he settled down to read but couldn't concentrate. Travis had been after him to buy a television set. Perhaps in April, Gus had replied.

He wandered the house. The kitchen needed painting. The sink was cracked. The faucets dripped. The bedroom his parents used was filled with boxes now: his mother's silver mirror-and-comb set, her perfume bottles, her wedding dress in a garment bag hanging on a hook in the closet; his father's set of *The Book of Knowledge*, missing two volumes; board games missing pieces, shop manuals for cars from his father's repair business. The Franklins weren't made anymore; the Oaklands were more or less Pontiacs now. A collection of Indian relics and old pennies. Bibles in various sizes. A stuffed pheasant, survivor of moths. A photograph album. He turned the pages: his parents in front of the hedge by the front steps, his father dressed in a suit and hat, his mother wearing a dress, hat, and gloves. Gus in sixth grade, baseball bat on his shoulder, fielder's mitt dangling from his belt. Where were his parents going? Where was the game?

Gus closed the door. In the other bedroom, the one where he'd always slept, he undressed, lingering at the window, listening to the sound of the wind.

He turned off the light and lay in bed, staring up at the ceiling, He had brought the envelope home, the one with the poem inside. The notepaper from Rubin's pad was in his jacket pocket. He got out of bed, found the poem and compared the paper it was typed on with Rubin's paper. They looked the same. They felt the same.

Where she had been. Past Elm, past Spruce, the golden goose, inquire within. She who? *Inquire?* Gus recalled Miss Page, his high school English teacher, telling him that years ago *inquire* meant to investigate, *enquire* meant to question in general, but only the English and some Europeans still distinguished between the two. He wondered if Rubin did.

"Enjoy yourself tonight?" Miss Harbaugh asked.

Her parlor was filled with hues of purple and rose. She lounged on a chaise in suede slippers, velvet trousers, and sheer blouse with a high ruffled neck. She smoked a cigarette in a black holder. There was a stemmed wineglass, nearly empty, on the table between her chaise and the armchair where Sheriff Pope sat smoking a thin Danish cigar, the kind that she was fond of smoking when she was by herself.

The guests had all gone home. Her ladies had retreated to their rooms to drink and talk and smoke as Miss Harbaugh and the sheriff were doing. The spirit lamp beside the wineglass cast an orange glow on the sheriff's pudgy hand as he reached for his own glass, whose contents he had poured from the silver flask he carried zipped into the lining of his official black leather jacket.

Pope was short and stout, like the teapot the ladies joked, referring to his spout as something surprisingly full grown.

"I'm sorry Milly's gone," Pope said. "I enjoyed her."

"They come, they go. But I would have expected she would tell me before she went. Tonight Miss Jewel did all right, didn't she?"

"Just fine."

Miss Harbaugh eased off the chaise and crossed the room. She returned with a painting. "I've just had it framed," she said. She held it up for Pope to look at. The nude stood by a window, the light slanting across her body. She was tall and angular, the breasts tipped with a color that reminded Pope of pomegranates, a fruit whose seeds he had loved to nibble when his mother had brought several home at Christmas for decorations.

"Not one of your girls, is she?"

"My no, much too young to join our little group. She's somebody painted from memory."

"Painted by that man who showed up here when school was starting again, end of summer?"

"Mr. Crim."

"He's got some memory."

"Which is to say he has some interesting things to remember." Miss Harbaugh leaned the painting against the wall and resumed her place on the chaise.

"How come you two hit it off?" Pope asked.

"He wanted to know about different people and I filled him in."

Pope stubbed out his cigar, leaned back, and sighed. "Milly was a picture I remember."

"At first I thought Bonnie would be your favorite."

"I tried her out a couple of times. She had her good points."

"Certainly more endowed than Milly. What was her appeal?"

"She was supple and subtle, blunt and honest."

"The last two I try to discourage in my ladies, at least in their dealings with guests."

Pope chuckled. "She called me conniving and corrupt. She was right. That's how I run a county and get things done, stay on top of things." Pope chuckled again. "Although around here I'm sometimes on the bottom, looking up. It was a pleasure to see Miss Milly looking down at me, with that smirk on her face." Pope took out his flask and added to his glass. "Any of your other guests fancy her?"

"Roy Hunt visited her a time or two. I let him do that even if I employ him. He set his brother up with her. Don't know how it turned out."

"Billy's not a regular, is he?"

"Sometimes he'd hang around and see if there was any work to do, but he wasn't a guest. He got no favors." Miss Harbaugh finished her wine.

The mantel clock chimed two.

"Sunday morning," Pope said. He swallowed the rest of his drink, stood up, and stretched.

"You really didn't mind Milly calling you conniving and corrupt?"

"Better than being called the conscience of the county, like some next door refer to Sheriff Salt."

"The other day he was over here."

"Upstairs?"

"We talked in the lobby. You recall that mute woman I had, he was asking about her. He speculated could be her bones in the hog pen."

Miss Harbaugh reached out and held Pope's arm. "You don't think it could be Milly, do you?"

"Milly could take care of herself."

The door closed. Miss Harbaugh poured a bit more wine and thought about Milly. There was a girl who asked too many questions and listened too carefully to the answers, like she was going to write everything down.

One must have a mind of winter
To regard the frost and the boughs
Of the pine-trees crusted with snow;

And have been cold a long time
To behold the junipers shagged with ice,
The spruces rough in the distant glitter

Of the January sun; and not to think
Of any misery in the sound of the wind,
In the sound of a few leaves,

III

Monday morning Gus patrolled until eleven. By then Miss Tolley had opened the library. Gus wondered how many beige skirts and gray blouses she owned. Today the building was chilly enough for her to add a blue sweater decorated with a white reindeer.

"Travis is really taking to poetry," she said.

"Here's one someone left for me."

Gus handed her the poem. She read it, shrugged, and gave it back. "What do you think?"

"Someone must be trying to tell you something."

"Yes, I got that far."

"Must be hundreds of towns with Spruce and Elm streets."

"Including Kingsville."

"So the writer suggests if you want to find this person, this *she*, where's she's been, you need to locate a certain golden goose and inquire within. Sounds simple enough."

"*Inquire*, as in investigate, you think? Not *enquire*?"

"Most people don't distinguish between them."

"My teacher did."

"Did you have Miss Page?"

"Never forget her."

"What difference does it make—*inquire* or *enquire*? It's not an esoteric clue. You're not Hercule Poirot. Either way you ask questions."

"You're probably right."

"Who is *she*?"

"No idea, but it might be a woman who wandered the county, sometimes riding a bike."

"I read about her and the fire. What about golden goose?"

"From the wording it's a place, don't you think?"

"I agree."

"In the middle of the night I decided a pawn shop."

"Then why are you here?"

"To use your German dictionary. I don't have one."

"Why German?"

"A hunch."

Gus followed Miss Tolley to the reference section. She took down a dictionary. Gus said, "This morning I remembered there's a little shop in Kingsville on Tanner Street with a sign that says Loans, between a business that rents wheelchairs and sells home-remedy products and a used-clothing store. You'd hardly notice the place, it's so small."

"Sheriff Gus, get to the point."

"I called around. A man named Gans owns the shop."

Miss Tolley thumbed the pages. "Gans is German for goose."

Gus smiled. "Thought it might be."

She pushed the dictionary into place on the shelf. "You're not in Poirot's league yet."

"Don't think he'd like it here," Gus said.

"What about you? Come April are you staying or leaving?"

"Hiding out."

He was still smiling when he returned to the office. Marla

had delivered Travis's lunch. She sat beside him and watched him spread mustard on his sandwich. Travis hadn't said anything, but Gus had the idea that Marla had fallen for him. And vice versa. "Need to get back," she said, smoothing her hand across Travis's shoulder.

"Bye," he said softly, then looked up at Gus. "Oh," Travis said. "Forgot, Mrs. Ross called in. Someone stole something. A towel, the one she showed you."

Gus shook his head and asked Travis for the keys to the deputies' cruiser. Twenty minutes later Mrs. Ross led Gus to Betty's empty room.

"I was away maybe an hour. My husband took the truck. He's not back yet. I decided to use the towel Betty made. I came to get it and hang it where I could admire it, and it was gone."

"Do you lock up?"

"Gracious, this is Harr County. If we remember, we lock the doors at night, never in the daytime."

"Do you think your husband might have moved the towel, put it somewhere?"

"Not Clifford. He never comes in here. Even if he did, the towel wouldn't interest him."

"And you've looked all over?"

"Once before I phoned your office and once again after I left your deputy my message."

"Anything else missing?"

"Nothing."

"When Clifford comes back, ask him anyway."

"Right now, I'm asking you. You're the sheriff, not Clifford." She sat down on the bed and picked at the coverlet. "I'm sure you don't consider a missing towel important, just some peculiar behavior, like last summer when someone stole

Mrs. Boone's underwear and her husband's overalls off her clothesline."

"That didn't amount to much, only some kids the Boones wouldn't let fish in their pond causing trouble. Your towel is connected to a missing woman who might have been murdered. It's important."

Gus left by the kitchen door and circled the house twice before getting in the cruiser and driving to Kingsville.

———∿∿∿———

THE BELL OVER THE DOOR TINKLED. Mr. Gans laid aside the catalog he was reading. A customer had just left. Gans had advanced him fifty dollars and taken a .45 Colt pistol for security and set it on the counter to tag and put away later. He wondered if the gun was why the Harr County sheriff was paying the shop a visit.

"Are you the owner?" Gus asked.

"Karl Gans, Sheriff. How may I help you?"

"I'm trying to locate a missing woman. The most striking thing about her is she couldn't speak. She worked awhile at the Johnson House and the Railroad Hotel. People called her Betty. Around thirty-five years old. Black hair, cut short. Green eyes. Medium height. A hundred and forty pounds, more or less. She usually carried a small green bag with her."

"She was here, months ago."

"How many?"

"Summer." Gans closed his eyes and thought for a moment. "Early July," he said. "Or late June." He picked up the catalog and put it on a chair behind him. "Definitely before August."

"Came here by herself?"

"No, no. A gentleman was with her."

"A person you do business with?"

"I'd not seem him before. A visitor to town, perhaps. He arrived in a taxi."

"Blue Cab?"

"We only have one."

Gus drummed his fingers on the counter. "Go on."

"The man did all the talking. He said the woman had some jewelry she wanted to sell. She took some pieces out of the green bag you spoke of. They were cheap costume items, nothing I wanted to deal with. That was it."

"Can you describe the man?"

"Heavy. Over six feet. Thick gray hair. Wore a brown suit like some of the salesmen who stay at the Johnson House wear. His summer hat had a yellow band. I liked that. The woman was in a dress of some kind. I recall it was short for wearing outside on the street. Probably cool enough though. You could practically see through it."

"Did you ever see her again?"

"Never."

"What about the man?"

"No."

Gus nodded toward the Colt. "Do you do a lot of business in guns?"

"Guns mostly, some jewelry, small antiques, books every now and then, and art."

"You don't display much in here."

"We're a small shop. I work deals with other traders. We take care of our own."

—⋘∿∿⋙—

"TRAVIS, ONE THING I'VE LEARNED IS when you ask a person to describe someone they don't want you to know about, they tell you the opposite of what the person really looks like."

"Mr. Gans told you the man with the mute girl was heavy, over six feet, with thick gray hair. So he's slight, short, and bald?"

"Could be."

"Could be several folks. You have anyone in mind?"

"Rubin Dazzle is about five-five, thin as a nail, and shaves his head. He also knew the mute. *Die stumme*, he called her."

Gus paced the office, rearranging the cactus twice. "You remember Bascombe Goodsell?"

"The antiques dealer Percy did business with?"

"When I entered Gans's shop, he was reading Bascombe's catalog. Gans said the mute wanted to sell jewelry, but he wasn't interested. The opposite could be true."

Gus found the keys to the old cruiser. "Phone Percy and ask him to contact Bascombe and say we need to speak to him. I have someone to see in Bow."

The afternoon sky full of dark clouds had no pity as far as Gus was concerned: more snow for sure. The cruiser needed a new thermostat. The heater wouldn't work, only blew cold air.

"You have coffee on your mind or more questions?" Bonnie asked.

"Both," Gus said.

Bonnie brought him a cup and leaned against the counter. "Fire away."

"I assume you know Miss Harbaugh at the hotel in Kingsville."

"She offered me accommodation."

"Did you accept?"

"I tried it out, but the situation didn't suit me. Too many rules. I like my independence."

"How long did you stay?"

"A month—Mothers' Day to Fathers' Day."

"Do you recall a mute woman working there?"

"The laundry lady. She came shortly before I left, after she was booted out of the Johnson House. Kind of snooty how she kept to herself, like she thought she was special. I heard from time to time she'd show a bit too much of herself to male guests. The manager of the Johnson House didn't care for that."

"Anything else?"

"Her eyes, green as glass, they looked right through you, like she could see into your soul and didn't much care for what she saw."

"How did Miss Harbaugh treat her?"

"Kindly."

"Did the woman have visitors?"

Bonnie squinted at Gus. "How do you mean that? She didn't entertain."

"Social visits. Someone she might have gone walking with, left the hotel with."

"The Thin Man. That's what Miss Harbaugh called him. She'd laugh about it. I think she took the name from a book she'd read. She does read right much. But the man was thin."

"Describe him."

"My height. Bald. He struck me as very proper. Or just shy."

"Did you hear him speak?"

"No, but I saw him pass a note to the woman and she passed one to him. When he shook hands with Miss Harbaugh, he gave a little bow. That's what I meant by proper. But I didn't hear if he said anything to her. If he'd come in the evening, I might have heard him."

The diner was almost empty. Bonnie filled the sugar bowls and wiped the counter. Gus drank his coffee.

"Roy Hunt works for Miss Harbaugh," Gus said.

"She lets him get away with too much. Thinks the girls should entertain him in their private time."

"What about Billy, his brother?"

"He wasn't around much. Sometimes Miss Harbaugh had a chore for him to do. He was only there because he'd lost his license and had to ride with Roy. Some of the girls said things about him, teased him."

"Why?"

Bonnie leaned closer and lowered her voice. "He was nervous. Liked to finish in a hurry. The girls called him Flash. Nothing like his brother."

"Nice talking to you," Gus said.

"I'm off tomorrow," Bonnie said.

"Chance of snow," Gus said.

"My place is warm. If you get cold, stop in and heat up."

Neva had dressed and sat at the table, watching Tony going through the sketches he'd made of her.

"Tony, how did you get out of France?"

"Eventually I made a deal. That's what we all did. Kessler had two valuable paintings the Germans wanted. I suggested how they might go about finding them."

"Any regrets?"

"We did what we had to do. I found my way to Canada,

then the States. The army handed me a uniform, gave me some basic training, and sent me back to Europe. The Germans found out I was good with a rifle. I had no regrets. They may have had some."

"What brought you here?"

"My painter's eye, the subtleties of the seasons changing. I was passing through, but the landscape spoke to me."

"Saying what?"

"Stay and paint."

Neva looked at her watch. "I wish I could stay. Even if I don't honor and obey, I cook supper, at least until Florry May gets back from tending family in Raleigh."

Tony helped Neva into her coat. "I saw you leaving the Railroad Hotel the other day," she said.

"I was looking for Milly."

Neva smiled. "I'm not enough for you?"

Tony kissed her cheek. "More than enough. When I first got to Kingsville, I met Milly at a bar over there. I had questions, she had answers."

"Like what?"

"Who welcomed strangers. Who didn't. And where I might find ladies who would pose for a price."

"And provide other services?"

Tony winked. "Never crossed my mind."

"But you're still thinking of Milly."

"I promised her one of the sketches."

"Does Milly have a last name?"

"Milly Hicks."

"Doesn't sound familiar. One of Miss Harbaugh's ladies?"

"She was. Not as pretty as the others, but the sheriff over there liked her. Some of the guests complained she was sarcastic and critical. Miss Harbaugh says she left town."

Tony walked Neva to her car and watched her drive away. Inside again he poured himself a glass of whiskey and sat down to drink it. He remembered the coal boat that brought him to Canada and the train to Montreal to get another train to the States and seeing a man he thought was Kessler because the Germans had joked about sending him there and following him to a dingy room where he had filled a chipped cup with brandy and handed it to Tony, complaining he was poor now and didn't have a clean glass for his guest. Newspapers covered the walls to keep out the chill, but it seeped through anyway.

Kessler sat on the bed. Tony sat on the chair. He reminded Kessler that the Hals and Holbein, both worth a fortune, would be waiting for him in Geneva when the war was over.

Then you know about that, Kessler had said. I overheard you telling my father about them, Tony said. The brandy was warming on a cold night in a cold room. Tony had sipped and smiled at his host. What else did you hear? Kessler asked. That Marie knew the code to recover the paintings, Tony answered, thinking to himself that the Germans he'd sent after her would have learned what it was and they had the paintings now, even Shüle's precious portrait of a woman who might not be alive anymore. The Germans were ruthless.

The code was hidden in a bracelet I gave her, but she didn't know that, Kessler said. Tony's smile vanished. How wrong he had been. He stated at Kessler. One day she will turn up, Kessler said. We will find each other. Now Kessler smiled. Tony stood and picked up the bottle to pour another drink. But you remember the code, don't you? Kessler nodded. Tell me, Tony said. The bottle was thick and heavy. No, Kessler said and kept on saying it even after the cup had dropped from his hand and broke, even after his blood spattered the walls.

———∿∿∿∿———

TUESDAY. BEFORE DAWN GUS HEARD THE plow clearing the road. At seven when Gus set out to walk to the cruiser, which he'd parked by his mailbox, his porch thermometer read nineteen degrees. The air was still, the sky full of stars. Only a few inches of snow. By noon the sun would be strong enough to melt most of it, he hoped.

Travis phoned the office to say he would be late. Duncan hadn't been back very long because the hood of the deputies' cruiser was still warm. The sidewalk hadn't been shoveled yet.

Gus stomped the snow off his shoes and shut the office door. "Coffee's ready," Duncan said.

"I think I'll retire to the Caribbean," Gus said and filled his cup.

"You speak any Spanish?" Duncan asked. "You'd need to down there."

"For sure I wouldn't need snow boots."

"Somebody from the county garage will be over soon to clean the sidewalk." Duncan handed Gus an envelope. "This was on the floor when I came in."

Gus opened the envelope and took out the piece of paper folded inside.

> *Blue is the man,*
> *That's her plan.*
> *In winter deep,*
> *The circle seek.*

Duncan read over Gus's shoulder. "What's that about?"

"Too much poetry," Gus said.

"Someone playing a joke on you? Travis maybe, or one of those that meet with Miss Tolley?"

Gus heard a shovel grating against cement and jumped up. Outside Mr. Dent was clearing the sidewalk, working his way down Lee Street from the garage to the office. Only two sets of footprints, Gus's and Duncan's. Gus waved to Mr. Dent, stomped the snow off again, sat down, and picked up his coffee cup.

"When did the snow start?" he asked.

"Around eleven."

"Not much help." Gus read the poem again. He remembered the figure in blue overalls on the towel. The person was digging in the ground. There was a plant or flower nearby, but Gus couldn't bring to mind what it looked like or what color it was. Then he remembered the sheet of paper Rubin had given him. He'd put it in a folder with the first poem."

"What do you think?"

Gus laid the three sheets on his desk. Duncan picked them up, thumbed them, and held them up to the light. "Appear the same," he said. "Where'd you get the blank sheet?"

"From Rubin Dazzle."

"If Spaid's store sells it, he's probably not the only person who has it. But you suspect it's him?"

"Duncan, I suspect he's pointing us in some direction, but it's up to us to figure where. It won't do any good to flat-out ask because he doesn't give flat-out answers."

—◦◦◦—

"MARKUS WEATHERS, NOW THERE'S A BLACK man who works hard," Hastings said.

Since he'd taken up residence and opened the chapel for regular services, he had begun the habit of eating his noon meal at Bowen's diner. Gus found it impossible to sit at the counter if there was an empty seat without Hastings sitting down beside him. Worse, if Gus sat at a table by himself, Hastings would join him without asking. At least at the counter Gus could stare straight ahead and not give much attention to whatever was on Hastings's mind.

Marla brought Gus's meatloaf sandwich and asked if he needed ketchup. No, Gus said. I do, Hastings said and lifted the bun off his hamburger. Marla took the bottle from her apron pocket and gave Gus a look of apology. Wasn't her fault if Hastings was a bother.

"All the months since the chapel had a regular priest, Brother Weathers has done a fine job keeping the property shipshape," Hastings said.

"He's a good man," Gus said.

"I heard he likes to drink."

"On occasion."

"But he's never caused trouble?"

"Absolutely not."

"I understand Reverend Pierce, my predecessor, drank."

Gus watched Marla spiral whipped cream over a hot-fudge sundae. "He did."

"I've spoken to his former wife. She doesn't seem interested in attending services."

"She never was."

Hastings wiped his mouth. "Ah," he said. "I thought perhaps it was only me she was avoiding."

"It's not personal."

"It's certainly personal to God, Sheriff. That I assure you. What do you think?"

"Are you asking what I think or what I believe?"

"For the moment—think."

"I think you should leave Ruth alone. Let her find her own way."

Hastings sighed and shook more ketchup out of the bottle for his french fries. "And you, Sheriff, are you finding your own way?"

"As best I can."

"Markus mentioned how sometimes he'd see you late afternoons sitting in the chapel by yourself."

"True," Gus said.

"I'm pleased to hear it. Since I arrived, one or two others have wandered in and sat in silence for a while. I believe we find our way to God through silence."

The silence of the grave, Gus thought and smiled to himself. Then he saw Marla and remembered her dropping a lily on her father's coffin.

"There was a young woman recently. I don't intrude upon people's solitude, but in her case I almost did. She stared upward with such devotion and rapture I wanted her to tell me what she saw."

"How long ago?" Gus asked.

"Those warm days in December."

"Did you speak to her?"

"Yes. I waited outside, but I only thanked her for being there."

"Did you ask her name?"

"I told her mine. Hers was Milly—Milly Hicks, I think. We

shook hands and she left."

"Did she have a car?"

"Of course. After all, it's quite a walk from town to Chapel Road."

"What make?"

"I don't know, Sheriff. I'm not up-to-date with my automobiles."

"Describe it."

"Small. Small and tan. Tiny, in fact."

"Have you ever heard of a Crosley?"

"Is that a car?"

"Small, like you described."

"News to me, Sheriff."

Gus finished his sandwich. "Did you see her again, this Milly?"

"Never again. I wish I had. I mean truly, Sheriff, I've never seen such an expression of utter rapture, as if she beheld God himself."

Gus paid his check and walked to the office. Bright drops of snowmelt dripped from roofs and trees. He phoned the DMV in Raleigh and told the clerk the plate number he had written on the sheet of paper Rubin had given him. The vehicle had recently changed owners. Bates Auto Auction in Kingsville had sold the car to Zeno Wooton.

Gus was about to drive to Ruffin when Bascombe Goodsell phoned. "I'm well acquainted with Mr. Gans," Bascombe said. "Primarily he runs a pawnshop. He lends money for things people bring him, things with some value—rings, watches, firearms, for example. However, from time to time folks bring him items of great value, often more than the owner knows, items they wish to sell, usually jewelry, but rare books and maps show up. Recently someone brought him a copy of Jefferson's *History of Virginia*, third edition, quite valuable.

"Understand Gans can't buy these items and turn around and sell them in King County or Harr County or most anywhere in the Piedmont. With the exception of Percy Levoy, there's not a market there. And Percy isn't acquiring much these days. So Gans offers me the opportunity to list special items in my catalog. I offer him a healthy return on whatever investment he's made."

"Is he honest?"

"Does he tell people what things are worth? Mostly he does."

"Mostly?"

"Let's say Mr. Gans and I might disagree sometimes about value. He tends to estimate low, I go high."

"When I showed up, he was reading your catalog."

"Yes, the autumn number. I mail it to my list the first week of August, but I call it the autumn catalog. Some real stunners in there."

"Any he passed on to you?"

"One, and just in time to add it, an art nouveau necklace— emeralds and tiny diamonds. When Gans first saw the piece, he was afraid the emeralds were alexandrites, but they weren't."

"Worth what?"

"Two thousand."

"Is it sold?"

"Not yet."

"Someone in King County or Harr County owned this necklace?"

"Gans had no reason to doubt ownership."

"Did he tell you who brought it in?"

"An older man and a woman. She was younger. He didn't tell me their names or much about them except the man did all the talking, like he was representing her. The necklace came from a Paris maker. Gans thought the man was European." Gus was silent for a moment. "Anything else?" Bascombe asked.

"Nothing," Gus said.

"What about Miss Blossom? Percy used to tell me what's going on with her, but we haven't communicated much lately. He usually found something in my catalog to peak his interest, especially if I had a Southern box of some kind to add to his famous box collection. Perhaps he's spending all his time on his new wife."

"Miss Blossom's writing movies now."

"She's pretty enough, she ought to be in them."

"I won't dispute that," Gus said.

Bascombe complained about the winter, how difficult his travels were, and said goodbye.

———

ZENO'S CLINIC CLOSED AT FIVE. At twenty after Gus knocked on the backdoor. Maggie let him in. She had changed out of her uniform and into a skirt and sweater and was putting on her coat. An easy day, she explained. The last patient had left at four thirty. For once she didn't give Gus a hard look. All through college they had dated, but Gus wasn't interested in marriage. Almost twenty years ago, a long time to hold a grudge.

She studied him. "You look older," she said. "You're not aging gracefully like I thought you would." She slammed the door behind her.

There was Zeno beside him, dressed in his usual working outfit: white shirt, green tie, khaki trousers, brown shoes with thick, soft soles. "What are you mumbling about?" he asked.

"I guess she isn't mellowing after all," Gus said.

"Guess not," Zeno replied. "You under the weather and need medical attention?"

"I was under the illusion you owned a Ford, but DMV tells me you also have a Crosley registered in your name."

"Not against the law to own two vehicles, is it?"

"Of course not, but why do you need two cars?"

"A Crosley only has two cylinders. I'd count it half a car."

"I've never seen you drive it."

"I don't. I lend it out. If one of my staff is having car trouble, I let the person use the Crosley. Sometimes a patient needs it to get around, meet appointments. Despite what you may believe, I can be very helpful." Zeno turned and Gus followed him into his office. Gus stood. Zeno leaned back in his desk chair, lit a cigarette, and tossed the match at the marble ashtray shaped like a heart.

"Help me," Gus said. "Who's using the car now?"

"No one."

"I saw it parked at Rubin Dazzle's place."

"That's where it's got to after Milly Hicks left it."

"Milly Hicks?"

"Sheriff, are you suffering hearing loss? Milly Hicks, yes, Milly Hicks. Get to the point."

"John Hastings mentioned her."

"The priest?"

"The very one. Where would I find Miss Hicks?"

"Sheriff, I honestly don't know. The gauge reads empty, so she ran out of gas on Girty Road. I assume someone gave her a ride or she walked, but don't know where. I haven't heard from her. Markus Weathers saw the car on the roadside Monday morning. He said he'd buy some gas and drive it back to the office. Monday was showery. Ice later. Snow after that, so the car isn't home yet. Frankly we've been too busy to get around to doing anything about the car."

"Why did Miss Hicks need it?"

"This time she said she was moving stuff, changing locations."

"This time?"

"Two Sundays ago, the fourth. She was one of my hotel girls. I assume she lived there. Where she was going, she never said."

"What about the first time?"

"She had the car over Christmas. Remember, it was warm then? She wanted to visit someone."

"Who?" Zeno shook his head. "Did you like her?"

Zeno reached across the desk and pulled the ashtray closer. "I like all my patients, and I try to respect their privacy."

"Except when you don't."

"When you push me for information and I give in."

"I'm merely asking in general."

"And I couldn't give you much specifics about Miss Hicks other than to say she was too thin in my estimation and went around with an ironic expression on her face as if she were judging you and you didn't grade out very well. Oh, and she didn't have a driver's license, she admitted that. But I let her use the car anyway."

"Good enough," Gus said. He moved toward the door. "Did she see a dentist?"

"I have no idea. What about you?"

"Doctor Keene in Levoy."

"No, I mean are you eating enough?"

"Winter takes away my appetite."

"Really? For most people it works the opposite. In winter they pile on the pounds." Zeno stubbed out his cigarette. "But as long as I've known you, you don't do as the rest of us do."

"Care to elaborate?"

"We're all on one big bus trying to get somewhere, like having more money or more friends or better reputations or jobs, but you, you're sitting in the back watching us. You don't care about destinations, only that we stay in our seats and behave."

"Sounds like a teacher on a school bus."

"Does, doesn't it?" Zeno chuckled. "Sheriff, you need recess time. Need to tell the driver to stop and let everyone off."

"And who is the driver?"

Zeno pushed the ashtray away. "I don't know. I got lost in my own metaphor. However"—he leaned forward and folded his hands—"you need to want something, desire something, or someone, that you can't live without. Like air. Something that completes you." Zeno looked at his watch. "Time to go home," he said. He took out his keys to lock up.

For a moment the two men stood in the parking lot in the dark and cold. "Is that where you're going?" Gus asked. "Home?"

"Those lingering summer afternoons are fine for visiting a friend and enjoying a drink or two before returning to one's hearth and a late supper—"

"Your friend being Maggie—"

"Don't interrupt. Winter is different. One's home is one's relief from the storm. One's abode is one's solace." Zeno eased himself into his car and looked up a Gus. "It may surprise you that I find pleasure in watching Neva toiling in the kitchen, or at least opening cans, pouring, stirring, and heating. Certainly surprised me."

One must have a mind of winter
To regard the frost and the boughs
Of the pine-trees crusted with snow;

And have been cold a long time
To behold the junipers shagged with ice,
The spruces rough in the distant glitter

Of the January sun; and not to think
Of any misery in the sound of the wind,
In the sound of a few leaves,

Which is the sound of the land
Full of the same wind
That is blowing in the same bare place

IV

Wednesday morning, a week since the hog pen had burned. Gus patrolled until noon, then he drove to Ruffin to avoid meeting Hastings at Bowen's diner.

"Didn't see you yesterday, Sheriff." Bonnie gave Gus a sly smile and handed him a menu. "Had the whole day to myself. Kinda lonely though. You know that feeling, like you yearn for a warm body to press against, relieve the emptiness of winter?"

Bonnie had lovely brown eyes and for a moment Gus felt keenly the yearning she was talking about. "I do," he said.

He held the menu but didn't look at it and ordered a chicken salad sandwich.

"Knew what you wanted before you sat down, didn't you?" Bonnie said and wrote the order on her pad.

She called the order into the kitchen and brought Gus a glass of water and napkin rolled around a knife and fork. "I suspect you also knew what you're going to ask me before you sat down. That's why you're here." The sly glance again, more a subtle rise at the corner of her mouth than a smile.

Gus unrolled the napkin and arranged the knife and fork in front of him. He wondered why spoons were so important he'd have to ask for one for his coffee.

"A woman named Milly Hicks, did you know her?"

"Some," Bonnie said. She went away to serve other customers. Gus could look into the mirror over the soda fountain behind the counter and watch the restaurant filling up. She came back with his sandwich.

"You want chips or anything?" she asked.

Gus shook his head. Zeno was right, he probably wasn't eating enough. She went away again.

Gus sat at the end of counter. A few of the other diners came over to say hello and ask how he was tolerating winter, but no one like Hastings wanting to sit beside him. He finished his sandwich and Bonnie poured his coffee.

"Milly showed up about the same time I did. Miss Harbaugh took a liking to her. Don't know where Milly came from, but I doubt she was from a farm family like most of Miss Harbaugh's flock. She may have had some college. She spoke well, but she had her opinions. She didn't shy from expressing them. Miss Harbaugh warned her about it."

Bonnie had five at the counter and two tables to wait on. The other waitress kept pushing her lank platinum hair into her hairnet and frowning at Bonnie to hurry her up.

Bonnie returned with a refill. "Did Milly have any visitors in particular?"

"The sheriff over there enjoyed her company. He likes 'em thin like Milly was so he can push 'em down and watch 'em squirm like they was prisoners or something. Milly was strong though. He liked that too, girls who didn't give in easily. I heard she packed up and went somewhere."

Bonnie took her time totaling Gus's check, leaning over the counter, the zipper of her uniform pulled down enough for Gus to see the rise of her breasts.

Gus left a generous tip. "Any idea where Milly might go?'

"None at all," Bonnie said. "Sometimes she and Betty would walk around Kingsville together."

"They were friends?"

"Seemed to be. Milly would say something, Betty would write her a note, and they'd laugh together."

Gus thanked Bonnie and started for the door. She called after him. "Sheriff, if you're in a visiting mood some night, don't be a stranger."

THE CROSLEY WAS STILL EDGED INTO RUBIN'S LANE. Gus sounded the cruiser's horn, and Rubin stepped out of his trailer.

"The car belongs to Zeno Wooten," Gus said.

"He's a busy man. I'm sure he'll fetch it when he has time."

"It's been here since Monday, nine days."

It's not an inconvenience, Sheriff."

"You said there was a note?"

"It may still be in my *mülleimer*—waste bin I think you call it. Should I look?"

"Tell me how you get around. I recall the first time we met. I parked on the road and walked up here to examine the place where a man had been shot and I found you."

"I was holding a serpent. You were most concerned."

"It was a copperhead."

"Correct."

"What I didn't find, or didn't notice, was any vehicle other than mine on the roadside. How did you get there?"

"A friend dropped me off. He returned later."

"Some local you knew?"

"No, an acquaintance from the city."

"Which city?"

"New York. While I—what is your expression?—got the lay of the land, my land just acquired from Mr. Levoy, my friend drove around awhile to get a sense of the county. We agreed it was very pastoral and peaceful and would suit me. I craved peace, my own private Eden, if you will."

"Yes, I remember your saying that."

"And now I am ordering my trees. Several varieties of apple, as you suggested. Serpents, as you also remember, I have plenty of."

Gus said, "See if you can find the note."

He watched Rubin walk back to the trailer, then bent down and peered into the car, aware that his back was stiff. He stretched, trying to loosen it. His shoulders hurt too. He leaned against the car and ran his hand over the top. He noticed streaks of blue paint.

Rubin returned and handed Gus the note. He recognized the writing.

"Rubin, I assume your friend has gone. How do you travel now? You said you liked eating at the Johnson House. How do you get around?"

"Blue Cab service in Kingsville."

"I thought you might use them," Gus said.

"Someone in Levoy ought to consider starting a convenience like that here."

"What about groceries?"

"Mr. Spaid delivers them."

"Books?"

"Mrs. Taylor phones and informs me what I might be interested in. She delivers too."

"I was told you attend Miss Tolley's poetry group."

"I went once. She picked me up and brought me home. Poe isn't Goethe. I was disappointed and declined to go again."

Gus took off his sunglasses and leaned against the car. "You and the mute girl we spoke of visited Mr. Gans's shop in Kingsville."

"The weather was warm then. I don't recall the exact date. Does it matter?"

"I'm curious about your transaction."

"The girl had noticed me and thought she could trust me. She had some jewelry to sell. I asked around and heard Mr. Gans was honest."

"Was he?"

"He gave a low appraisal of the pieces, but Betty, as people referred to her, accepted what he offered. She put the proceeds into the little green bag she carried, and we returned to the Johnson House." Rubin stared at the ground. "I'm not sure what else to say."

Gus considered mentioning that Betty was staying at the Railroad Hotel when she and Rubin had met Mr. Gans. Instead he put on his sunglasses and opened the driver's door of the Crosley. Gum wrappers stuffed the ashtray, the glove compartment empty except for a few receipts for repairs. A length of rope lay coiled on the gritty floormat. Gus shut the door. Rubin followed him to the cruiser.

The two men stared at each other as if one was expecting a question and the other was considering how to ask it. "Nothing," Gus mumbled, took off his hat, gathered himself into the cruiser, and drove back to the office.

"Did he tell you anything?" Travis asked.

"Some of what he did tell me isn't true, and I'm sure he knows I know it, which amounts to telling me something's true."

"I'm lost. Spell it out."

"Betty's bicycle was tied to the roof of the Crosley. Hicks was delivering the bike to Rubin. The Rosses haven't seen Betty since Christmas. Roy claims to have seen her New Year's Day. I guess I believe him. I also guess delivering the bike to Rubin was a message that she was okay. And he put it out where someone would see it and tell me and I would start looking for her." Gus paced the room. "Then there's the little verses I'm sure he wrote, little clues to keep me going."

"Why's she hiding?"

"Don't know."

"And where?"

"Don't know. But we do know the bones aren't hers."

"Whose are they?"

"Milly Hicks—probably."

"Who killed her?"

Gus took the note out of his pocket. "Don't know that either."

———

THE TWILIGHT DEEPENED INTO DARK, SQUEEZING the last streaks of light out of the sky.

Maggie owned a cottage on South Street, an area of spreading trees and wide lawns several blocks from the center of Kingsville. Gus parked the old cruiser behind a new Plymouth. He hoped she didn't have company.

Wilted liriope edged the brick path from the street to the front steps. He rang the bell. Maggie opened the door and stared at him. He held up the note Rubin had given him.

"You better come in," she said.

She wore a long purple robe and pulled the sash tighter.

Barefoot, she noiselessly followed Gus down the hall, a ghost of past assumptions and mistakes. "Here," she said.

The room was handsomely paneled, the wide pine floor sanded and stained the color of pale honey. Oriental rugs were arranged here and there. Gus recognized several lamps and tables he had seen years ago in Maggie's parents' house. Both dead now, her mother had collected antiques. Her father, Dixon Reems, a lawyer, was twice Kingsville's mayor. He had left Maggie enough money to live comfortably.

"I recognized your writing," Gus said.

She stood facing him, silent, as if collecting her thoughts, scanning his face, as if collecting his.

"Bourbon or Scotch, I have both," she said.

"Bourbon," Gus said. He watched her pour whiskey into two glasses on the colonial side table by the highboy in the corner of the room. She did live comfortably.

She handed him his glass. "Let's sit," she said and placed two coasters on the table in front of the couch facing the fireplace. She sat down and took a long sip of her drink.

Gus said, "You knew I would, didn't you?"

She kept her gaze on the firedogs. "Are you referring to your rejecting our long and deep carnal relationship, which I considered, in my psychological innocence, more enduring than the ephemeral college romance you assumed it to be, or something else?"

"You knew I would recognize your writing."

"Perhaps."

"Perhaps you were sending me a message."

"And what would that be?"

"Something to do with Milly Hicks." Maggie leaned back and closed her eyes. "Tell me," Gus said.

"No, you tell me first."

"She was driving the car that's in Rubin Dazzle's lane where you and Markus Weather left it. Miss Hicks seems to be missing. What should I know about her?"

"What do you know already, besides she's missing?"

"What does anyone know? She appeared in Kingsville one day, lingered with Miss Harbaugh for a while, then left. She was physically slim and mentally sharp, a bit too much so for some people. Zeno let her use the Crosley to move her stuff. Where is her stuff? Where was she moving it to? Who was the last person to see her? When? Where? Etcetera. Oh, there was a bicycle on top of the car."

"If Markus saw it when he found the car Monday morning, he didn't tell me. I didn't see it when we got back." Maggie said.

"Slow down. Got back when?"

"Mondays I always get to the clinic early, tidy the waiting room, water the plants, make sure we're prepared for another week of folks wanting relief from the flu going around. Markus starts early too. He told me about seeing the Crosley, and we went back to push it off the road. It ran out of gas close to where Mr. Dazzle lives. So we pushed it into Mr. Dazzle's lane and left a note. After that we drove to the clinic. Winter hours, we don't open until nine thirty."

"I didn't realize Markus works there."

"Zeno hired him to build some shelves. Sometimes he gets to the clinic before anyone else."

Gus stood and straightened the painting above the fireplace: a county lane and willow trees in spring.

"Anything in the car? Any of the things Miss Hicks was moving?"

"Nothing I saw."

"Just fields over there. Where was she going? Or where wasn't she going?'

Maggie watched Gus adjust the picture again. He didn't used to be like that: fussy, as if everything was slightly off, out of place. Marrying him and watching him change—they wouldn't have stayed together. Now he was staring down at the cold hearth.

"Maggie…"

He looked down again and didn't finish his sentence. Years and years since she'd heard him softly speak her name.

"What?" she asked.

"I need you to show me where you found the car."

"Gus, it's seven o'clock. It's winter. It's dark. Tomorrow?"

"You work tomorrow. Get dressed. We'll drive over there, and you show me where on the road you found the car."

"Gus, can't you ask Mr. Dazzle?"

"I'd rather spend time with you."

Maggie set her glass next to Gus's on the table. "Gus…I don't know what to say."

"Get dressed."

"You used to like the opposite."

"Maggie, I'm sorry but—"

"Gus, I can tell you where the car was. Stay here. You haven't touched your drink."

Gus sat down again. Maggie handed him his glass. "Your hands are cold," she said.

"I'm not a winter person."

She was going to suggest warmer clothes, but there wasn't any point. More than his skin was cold.

She said, "About fifty yards from Mr. Dazzle's mailbox, the

row of pines, what's left of the ones Percy planted when he decided to beautify the road, that's where the car was."

"Okay," Gus said. "I'll look around tomorrow." He tasted his whiskey, put the glass on the table, and stood up again. "Thanks for the drink."

Maggie sat very tense and still, holding her glass in her lap with both hands. "Gus, do you recall my father?"

"Yes."

"You know my father did some legal work for Percy Levoy?"

"Yes."

"When my father died, I left his files for Mr. Hudson, who took over the practice. I kept some letters. There's one I want to show you."

She was only gone a minute. *Twelve Trees, October 1938.* The ink had faded, but the words were clear enough: *Dear Mr. Reems, Regarding the situation of the late Jeremiah Salt, I believe his son, who is about to enter college, does not need to know, not yet. The money will be waiting. Your friend, P. L.*

"Do you want to sit down and finish your whiskey?"

"Do you want me to sit down and speculate about what I didn't need to know?"

"Gus, for a long time I've debated whether or not to give you the letter. I finally decided the time had come, and this evening turned out to be convenient. I'm planning to sell the house and move away. I'll leave the speculating to you."

"But some thoughts have crossed your mind."

"Gus, what I think doesn't matter."

Gus sank into the sofa again and picked up his glass. "Why are you leaving?"

Maggie reached out her hand and spread her fingers. "Let

me count the reasons." Her fingers closed around Gus's hand. "But I won't. Mostly I'm tired of being Zeno's lover and he's tired of me. I need to see new faces and make new friends. I don't want to grow old here."

"You're only forty."

"Tell that to yourself."

"Where are you going?"

Maggie leaned sideways, her cheek pressed against a cushion. "One day San Francisco, but right now to the kitchen if you'd like something to eat." She waited for Gus to answer. "Otherwise I think I'll sit and enjoy more whiskey and you can let yourself out."

At home Gus opened the rolltop desk that had been his father's and took out the tin box of letters that his mother had saved. He added the letter Maggie had given him to the others. The new letter confirmed what Gus had suspected.

He cooked himself a pork chop. He had run out of canned beans, so he opened a jar of applesauce. Maggie would have fed him better, but he didn't want company. Her whiskey was better than his as well, but he poured himself a glass. He ate his supper and poured himself another.

———

THURSDAY MORNING WAS COLD AND CLEAR. Travis was eating the breakfast Marla had delivered from the diner. "Got news," Travis said as soon as Gus walked in the door.

Travis poured syrup on his biscuit. "I asked Duncan if he'd heard of Milly Hicks. Turns out one night he pulled her over on Girty Road. Didn't cite her, so we didn't see her name on anything."

Gus waited while Travis chewed and swallowed. "Just after Christmas, Duncan was patrolling and she was driving that little car and he saw her turn onto Girty Road and her brake light showed like she was going to drive up where Mr. Dazzle lives, but she suddenly turned completely around and was heading in the opposite direction directly toward Duncan. He blinked his lights, didn't need the siren, and she stopped. He got out to warn her to slow down. She apologized, saying she'd forgotten something she needed and wasn't paying attention. Duncan said while they were talking he noticed a Jeep pull out down the road past Dazzle's place and drive away. Didn't have its lights on. Duncan said Miss Hicks acted nervous, scared like, but when the Jeep disappeared, she seemed relieved."

Gus poured himself a cup of coffee and watched Travis finish his meal. "How many Jeeps in the county?"

"Three I can think of," Travis said. "Mine, Mr. Conroy's, and Piney Nix's." Travis refilled his own cup. "You reckon it's Piney?"

"I do. I wouldn't put it past him to be keeping an eye on Rubin, planning something against him, but why would Piney concern Milly Hicks? Zeno said she was one of Miss Harbaugh's hotel ladies. Unless Piney was a customer, did she even know him? She spent her time in King County."

"You're thinking she thought the Jeep belonged to someone there?"

"I am."

"I can think of one man who drives one."

"Pope?"

"About the same beat-up condition as Piney's. But why would Pope be parked off Girty Road?"

"I doubt he would be, but I'm not sure what Miss Hicks thought."

Gus rinsed his cup and put it away. Twenty minutes later he parked by the five pines remaining from the row of twenty Percy had planted along the fence years before he sold the property to Rubin Dazzle. The lower branches were cut off. Bits of No Trespassing signs stuck to some of the trees. The rusty fence had come unnailed from the trunks and lay mostly covered by weeds and brambles.

Gus found some partial shoeprints and tire marks, the narrow ones probably from the Crosley, but nothing of much use. He walked up and down the roadside, then back and forth in the swale between the road and the trees. Close to the fence bits of thread stuck to the blackberry bramble, and a patch of weeds lay flat as if someone had rolled in them. He pulled them apart and found a silver chain thin as thread. He slipped it into his pocket, walked up the road, and knocked on Rubin's door.

He peeped out. Gus pushed the door wider. "The woman driving the Crosley—Milly Hicks—you'd seen her before." Rubin didn't answer. "That's not a question," Gus said. "Miss Hicks and *die stumme*, as you call her—Betty as others do—the two of them knew each other, and Betty introduced you to Milly and you agreed to help her. I'm sure Hicks was on her way to see you one night when she saw something that spooked her, and she turned around and left. I suspect she was on her way here again when she ran out of gas and something happened."

"Something happened?"

"She disappeared."

"Sheriff—"

"Rubin, am I right?"

"Probably."

"What's 'probably' about what I said?"

"You don't have proof anything happened."

"Rubin, we're not having a metaphysical debate here. I know I'm right."

"Good we're not because demanding you're right doesn't make it so."

"Damn it, Rubin. One woman is missing. Something happened to her."

"Two women isn't it?"

Gus stared at Rubin. "One, not two. The mute is alive. One day she'll be riding that bicycle again, the one you left where somebody would see it to keep us on her trail—not to mention you leave me little verses, little puzzles to work out."

Rubin looked up at the sky. "Quite a lovely day for working things out. However," he shrugged, "winter is not a happy season for you."

"It's not." Gus started to leave but hesitated. "Rubin, do you own a gun?"

"Why do you ask?"

"Because you've seen footprints from someone walking around your trailer at night, because someone has been parking down the road at night, and, most of all, because you know hate firsthand and might feel the need to have a weapon."

"Sheriff, my only weapon is my words."

"Rubin, you speak several languages. Your English is excellent. But all of that isn't enough, and you know it."

"Sheriff, you certainly have strong opinions about what I know and don't know."

"Rubin, I have a strong opinion that I don't know you very well."

Rubin smiled. "Perhaps we are having a metaphysical

debate after all. What do we know? What can we know? What do we need to know?"

Gus walked back to his cruiser. The sun was warmer now. He drove to the Newsome farm. Mrs. Newsome kept her grip on Sparky's collar. Yes, the chain on the Lucky Lindy was like the one Gus held out to her. Too bad he didn't find the medal instead of the chain. What good was it, broken like it was.

She complained about unwanted visitors. "It's been a week now, and folks are still wanting to see whatever they think there is to see. I had to visit Kingsville the other day, and someone dug up a couple of plants while I was gone.'

"Show me," Gus said.

Mrs. Newsome snapped a leash on Sparky's collar. Past the chicken house there was a mimosa tree, and nearby two plants had been uprooted and put back.

"Easy to see what someone did," Mrs. Newsome said. "When the ground thaws, I'll work soil around 'em and they'll probably live." Sparky raised his leg and urinated.

"What kind of plants are they?"

"Wet ones now. Betty transplanted them from the field somewhere. Black-eyed Susans, I think. Not sure." Mrs. Newsome poked the dirt with the toe of her boot. "Guess she'll not be around to tell me."

———

PINEY HANDED ROY THE HAMMER AND held the ladder while Roy climbed it and nailed the sheet of plywood to the beam under the roof. Roy climbed down and the two men hunkered under a tree by a stack of used tires. Each had a thermos of coffee. They drank and smoked.

"Taking shape nice," Roy said. "Come spring, you ought to be open for business again."

"Suppose so," Piney said.

"You don't sound enthusiastic."

"I'm not. I quit fixing cars 'cause I don't like getting all greasy and nicked up and having folks complain I took too long or charged too much. When I made the station into a store and only kept the tire and gas business, folks expected me to give 'em credit and act grateful for trading with me, or some got snooty 'cause of the Trade with the Klan sign I stuck to the door. Hell, the sheriff wouldn't set foot inside. A bunch of others felt the same. I didn't go around burning crosses or anything. I was just being neighborly."

"When you open again, you going to hang out another Klan sign?"

Piney flicked his cigarette into the weeds and spit. "I am. If people don't want to trade with me, they don't have to. Don't need 'em, don't want 'em. What I like is sitting outside on a summer morning and discussing events with neighbors who share my point of view while we feast on catfish I fried up and a big ripe melon fresh from the field and hushpuppies steaming from the stove."

"I guess I'd like that too."

Piney stood and bushed the pine needles off his overalls. "Roy, you could work for me, work days and keep your nights free for Miss Harbaugh."

"Not sure, Piney. I have leaving the county on my mind."

"Moving over to King County?"

"More like moving out of state. South Carolina or Florida."

"Why?"

"No more reason than the urge to wander."

"What about Billy?"

"He'd go with me."

They walked past the gas pumps. Roy picked up the hammer and ran his hand over it. "I never see much of Billy anymore," Piney said.

"When he's not working for Tuft's, he sticks to himself."

"I heard he liked to tour the countryside in that Mercury of yours, speeding and sipping."

"The sheriff took his license away."

"Too much speeding?"

"Too much of both."

"I bet you know a lady or two at Miss Harbaugh's that would fix ol' Billy up."

"He visited once or twice. He's shy. Ladies make him uneasy. They tease him some, call him Flash."

"Roy, it's a truth I've learned—desire finds us early, but it takes time and patience to learn how to use it. Maybe all your brother needs is practice."

"Maybe."

Piney bent down and lifted another sheet of plywood. Roy helped him line it up and nail it. "What about you?"

"Miss Harbaugh lets me work there. She doesn't let me sport there."

Piney laughed and squeezed Roy's shoulder. "I bet you do though."

"It's happened."

"What about Wooton? I've heard some of Miss Harbaugh's ladies visit him. He ever visit them?"

"Not I'm aware of."

"What about that Jew man—Dazzle?"

"Like I told you before, I only saw him once when he

visited the mute. Never took him to be a customer."

Piney snickered. "Maybe the Krauts cut off his manhood."

"Did they do that?"

"Why do you think them guard dogs looked so well-fed?"

Roy winced and slid another piece of plywood off the pile. "I was too young to know much about that war."

"We had a Jew president. We didn't need to send our boys to die overseas."

"Roosevelt was a Jew?"

"Does Roosevelt sound like an American name to you? If he wasn't, he was in with them, those Eastern-money types."

Roy nailed the plywood into place.

"Tell you one thing," Piney said. "Those Germans had some good ideas when it came to controlling their population. We could learn from them. Blacks, misfits, Communists, defectives, homos—too many of them around. Bad for the economy. Bad for society."

Roy nodded and rubbed the hammer against the leg of his jeans.

———

"A MAN LEFT THIS FOR YOU." Travis handed Gus the envelope.

"Another poem?"

"Too big for that."

Gus slit the envelope open. "Dental records. Did the man give his name?"

"Nope. Only said you'd be interested."

Gus took a deep breath and pointed to the patient's name: *M. Hicks.*

"You ever seen the man before?"

"No. He gave me the envelope and said to show you. I didn't ask his name and he didn't tell it, but he acted friendly and we walked outside. He drove a black car with a state tag."

"He wanted you to see the car."

"Could be."

"Could be we have proof who the victim was."

"Then why didn't the man give it to that state person—Grogan—who was here before?"

"Because he wanted me to know the state is involved without coming right out and saying so. Someone in the system knows the bones are Hicks's. Someone in the system knows more about her than we know and we're supposed to catch up."

"There's more to this than they want to tell us?"

"Tell us officially, yes."

"So now we're working for them?"

"What we find out they add to what they know."

"Why not just tell you what they know?"

"For some reason they want to pretend the state isn't involved."

"Why?"

"We can go where they don't want to be seen going? To deny being involved if something goes wrong?"

"If the bones are Hicks's, then what?"

"We keep it to ourselves."

Travis sat down and watched Gus relocate the cactus. "Okay, Mrs. Newsome said the chain you found was from her medal. You believe that?"

"I do."

"What else?"

"Mrs. Newsome gave the medal to Betty, but I don't think she lost it in the weeds."

"Who did?"

"Probably Milly Hicks. She was being followed. She tried to get to Dazzle's trailer. She ran out of gas. The person following her pulled her out of her car. They struggled, rolled around in the grass. Then person took her somewhere, cracked her skull, and laid her body in a hog pen that was set to be burned."

"How would the person know that?"

"Precisely."

"And how did the person put the body there?"

"If you can answer the first question, you'll probably answer the second."

"The vet knows about hog disease and tells people that Mrs. Newsome's hogs are infected and need to be killed and the pen burned down."

Gus nodded. "Go on."

"He's likely to tell people at Tuft's store."

Gus kept nodding.

"If the store delivered some watering troughs to the Fisk's farm, the body could have been on the truck."

"Mr. Ross said the Fisks were away when the troughs were delivered. No problem to get the body to the pen and lay it where Mrs. Newsome starting the fire wouldn't see it."

"Who are we talking about?"

"Billy Hunt," Gus said.

Tony handed the bracelet to Neva. "One of my models used to wear it. I asked her to take it off when we worked. It distracted me. One day she left it behind."

"And you kept it?"

"I thought she'd come back. She didn't. She was fidgety, so I didn't care. For some reason I held on to the bracelet."

Neva stood by the window and tilted the bracelet to the light. "I don't imagine it's worth very much."

"Not much at all."

Tony wrapped his arms around Neva and kissed her neck. "You can keep it if you want it."

"I'll take you instead."

"What about Europe? I've been thinking of going back. I'd like to take you with me."

Neva leaned her forehead against the window. "Gracious."

Tony worked his hands down her body. "Gracious yes or gracious no?"

"Gracious, I'll need to think." She reached for his hands and held them still. "Tony, do you really care for me?"

"I do."

"When would you leave?"

"Spring in Paris is a treat."

"April?"

"'April in Paris, chestnuts in blossom'... forgot the rest."

"Leaving Zeno would change everything. It's a big step."

"Haven't you already left him?"

"You've never been married."

"What difference does it make?"

"There are connections that run deep. When they're broken, there's a lot of pain, deep pain no matter how smooth everything appears on the surface."

"I feel deeply about you."

Tony's answer felt easy, practiced, flaccid, even if she could feel he wasn't. Neva eyed their faces in the glass. "We're talking to our own reflections."

"I did a painting like that once."

"Lovers?"

"Yes."

"What happened to them?"

"They lived happily ever after."

"Did you paint that?"

"I couldn't figure out how."

Neva turned and kissed him and picked up her coat. "I need some time."

"We have weeks."

"Let's see how it plays out."

At the door Tony kissed her again, then watched her drive away. He had what he needed: the bracelet, the numbers. Willing women weren't a necessity, just a convenience.

He closed the door and poured himself a glass of wine. He had to travel miles to find a decent bottle. The local taste seemed to run to bad wine and local whiskey that he could hardly swallow. At least in Kingsville you could buy a good drink. Having a corrupt sheriff had advantages.

And he had traveled miles for Betty. Betty—what a ridiculous name, so cheap, so common. Marie DeVris Kessler had been expensive and rare. The saucy Marie admiring herself in the mirror, who could forget the image? The scornful Marie. The insolent Marie. Look but don't touch.

Pity if she had perished in, of all places, the abode of swine. In the first weeks Tony had been in Kingsville and made the acquaintance of Miss Harbaugh, he had heard stories of Betty's wanderings and sudden flashes of flesh. Perhaps she had revealed herself to the wrong man and paid the price. Tony knew what men were capable of. He knew what he was capable of. He had been prepared to kill her himself, but that hadn't been necessary. Of course years earlier he had betrayed her, set the German agents to find her and get what she knew out of her. They had never met, and now it didn't matter whether she was alive or dead. He had what he'd come for, the bracelet, thanks to a cold night in Montreal and the nosy reporter Mrs. Newsome let see Betty's room and to whom she had praised Betty's sewing skills. In his story the reporter singled out the towel: the cherubic farmer in blue overalls holding his shovel by a tree—a mimosa like the one behind the house, Mrs. Newsome said. Betty loved planting flowers. Rubin must have seen Tony and recognized him. Betty had heeded Rubin's warning and buried the bracelet. If something happened to her, the scene on the towel would tell Rubin what she'd done. Such a shame she couldn't talk.

Tony folded the sandpaper he'd bought at Spaid's store into a tiny square and began to rub it back and forth across the bracelet. The plastic veneer disappeared. The tiny numbers beneath appeared. Geneva in April, not Paris. But he didn't have time to wait that long. Geneva in January would do. He couldn't wait for Neva to make up her mind. He'd already waited long enough.

One must have a mind of winter
To regard the frost and the boughs
Of the pine-trees crusted with snow;

And have been cold a long time
To behold the junipers shagged with ice,
The spruces rough in the distant glitter

Of the January sun, and not to think
Of any misery in the sound of the wind,
In the sound of a few leaves,

Which is the sound of the land
Full of the same wind
That is blowing in the same bare place

For the listener, who listens in the snow,
And, nothing himself, beholds
Nothing that is not there and the nothing that is.

"The Snow Man"
~ by Wallace Stevens ~

V

"Neva not feeding you?"

"Got a late start this morning," Zeno said. "Neva was sleeping."

The clock over the shelf of cups and glasses read nine. If Zeno wanted breakfast, the Nook was closer to the clinic than Bowen's. Gus decided Zeno had something to tell him.

"You're not eating much," Gus said.

"A biscuit and coffee are enough to keep me going."

Marla brought Gus an order of eggs and sausage. "Neva all right?" Gus asked.

"Her painter wants to take her to Paris."

"Is that where he's from?"

"Once was. He arrived here from Philadelphia."

Gus buttered his toast. "Was she asking your permission to go?"

"She asked me how I felt about it. I said I'd rather she didn't."

"But you didn't tell her no."

Zeno watched Gus cut his sausages into tiny pieces and arrange them on one side of his plate.

"I've never told Neva *no* about anything. She's never told me *no* either."

"If she went, would she come back?"

"Who can say? I don't think she can."

"Does she want to go?"

"She's flattered he asked her."

"But does she want to go?"

"What do you think?"

"I think she wants you to show her you don't want her to go."

Zeno lit a cigarette and watched Gus eat forkfuls of egg and sausage. "That's what I thought."

"Did you do anything?"

"I said life wouldn't be the same without her."

"That's not saying you can't live without her."

"She knew what I meant."

Gus finished his toast. He said, "Then she must know how to read between the lines."

Zeno stubbed out his cigarette. "Maggie's leaving."

"I know. She told me."

"You two made up?"

"I stopped by the other night. She gave me a letter."

"Did she talk about me?"

"She talked about moving on, not growing old in Harr County."

Zeno took out his wallet and laid a five-dollar bill on top of the check Marla had left on the counter.

"Gus, is that what we're going to do, you and me, grow old in Harr County?"

"Right now I don't see a way around it."

"Come April you might see differently. You filled out the law school application yet?"

"Too much on my mind."

"In my case, too little on my mind. Wherever I turn I

always find Neva."

"Tell her that. Tell her you want to keep it that way."

Zeno buttoned his coat. "Gus, for all your faults, sometimes you say what people need to hear."

Gus heard the door close behind him and asked Marla for another cup of coffee.

———

TRAVIS HAD CONTACTED GROGAN AND GIVEN him the dental records. Now he brought them back. No doubt about it, the deceased was Millicent Hicks. He agreed not to release the information. The *Lantern* reporter was sure the bones were Betty's and that's what most people believed, what Gus wanted them to believe.

After lunch Gus phoned Bascombe Goodsell again to ask how many people in Philadelphia received his catalogs. Fifteen for sure, Bascombe said. He'd have to check his list to give an exact number.

Check for a Tony Crim, Gus said. Don't need to, Bascombe said. He explained that Tony's father had owned a gallery in Paris. When he died, Tony had taken it over, then the Germans showed up. They allowed him passage to Canada. Eventually he returned to the U.S. and joined the army. He painted and had a bit of money to get by on, but not enough to satisfy his taste for important art and pricey antiques. He couldn't afford to buy much, but he was always interested in what Bascombe's catalog offered for sale. The emerald necklace Bascombe had mentioned before, Tony had phoned Bascombe to ask about it, how he had acquired it, what was its history—to use a fancy term, its provenance.

Bascombe added that Tony was a good-enough artist in his own right, though his portraits were a bit too fleshy for Bascombe's taste.

On the fifth try, the old cruiser (provenance Detroit 1939) started as if it preferred being parked in the afternoon sun to another trip to Girty Road.

Gus found Rubin walking his property, planning where he would plant each tree. The coat he wore over a wool sweater was worn at the elbows. Briars stuck to his twill trousers. "Earth tones," he said. "Appropriate for planting, don't you think?"

"I was thinking of something else," Gus said. "The Crim gallery?"

"Yes, I knew it. On Rue Lepic, very near Rue Ravignan where so many painters lived. Are you interested in art, Sheriff?"

"I'm interested in Tony Crim."

"Sylvester's son—Sylvester Crim. Most people called him Sy, but Sylvester was his given name."

"Did you meet Tony?"

"I don't believe so."

"The painter you see wandering the county is Tony Crim."

"How extraordinary. If I encounter him, I'll introduce myself. All of us must dine together."

"Food for thought," Gus said. "Mr. Crim inquired about a necklace you and Betty brought to Mr. Gans in Kingsville. You weren't entirely truthful about the quality of what she had to sell. The item is offered in a catalog put out by a man I know, Bascombe Goodsell."

Rubin rubbed his hands together. "It's turning chilly again, Sheriff. Perhaps you could make your point."

"Crim is here for a reason, which has something to do with the necklace or the woman or both."

"Perhaps the next time you see him you should ask."

"Rubin, who is the woman?"

"Sheriff, you know—"

"Betty—what's her name, her real name?"

"Find her, Sheriff, and I'll tell you."

The two men stared at each other. "I will," Gus said and walked back to the cruiser.

Travis was finishing for the day. Duncan was brewing a pot of coffee for his thermos. Travis put on his coat and picked up his poetry book. Gus looked at his watch, brushed past Travis, and ran out the door.

On winter afternoons Spaid's store closed at five. Five minutes to spare. "Bicycles?" Gus shouted at the only clerk he saw. The girl pointed toward the sporting goods section. Ted Spaid came out of his office and followed Gus to the back of the store.

"Gus, catch your breath."

"Bicycles."

"Yes, I heard you shout when you came in. You want to buy a bicycle and can't wait until morning?"

"I want to find out if you sold any bicycles lately."

"We keep three or four in stock. We hardly ever sell one. Even kids seem to have cars now, or friends with cars. But a few days ago Ruth Pierce—no, Ruth Levoy she is—bought a girl's Schwinn. I helped her load it into her car." Ted stared at Gus. "Sheriff, you're smiling like you just won the Irish sweepstakes."

The diner wasn't closed yet. Gus treated himself to the chicken cordon bleu, or Bowen's version of it.

⸻

THE NEXT MORNING GUS ASKED TRAVIS to do a foot patrol around the shops on Main Street and radio him if he saw Ruth Levoy.

Gus had stopped on the Ruffin Road to help a farmer repair a flat tire when Travis reported that Ruth was buying groceries. When Gus arrived, her car was still in Spaid's parking lot. Travis had followed her around the store and told Gus he'd overheard her tell the butcher she needed a roast big enough to serve five.

Gus opened the door of Percy's Buick for Ruth to set her groceries on the back seat. "Let's see," Gus said, "you, Percy, Teddy, Mrs. Ravenel—that's four. The roast serves five. Am I invited?"

Ruth opened her mouth to speak but didn't say anything.

"Of course, Teddy's new caretaker," Gus said. "Guess I'm not invited after all."

Ruth recovered. "Gus, we're not entertaining much these days. The winter's been hard on Percy."

"As I recall, heating a house as old as Twelve Trees is difficult. Old bones don't like cold."

"You're right, they don't."

"Percy mentioned the new woman—Alice he called her."

"Marie," Ruth said.

"Which is it?"

Ruth frowned. "Marie," she hesitated, "Percy gets confused. Marie French."

"Is she French?"

"I don't know. I haven't asked. She—"

"Doesn't speak?"

Ruth's mouth fell open again.

"What color is her new bicycle? The old one was blue."

"Gus, why all these questions?"

"Because I want one answer. The missing girl that folks believe burned up is living at Twelve Trees. Yes or no?"

Ruth leaned against the car and pressed her head against her arm. "Oh, Gus—"

"Ruth, look at me."

She turned around. "Yes."

Gus tipped his hat. "The *Almanac* predicts an early spring. Percy will like that. I know I do."

Gus suddenly felt tired. His body ached.

"You all right?" Ruth asked.

"Don't know," he answered, but he did know.

"Get some rest," Ruth said.

At home Gus considered warming some soup, but he lay down instead and shivered. One blanket wasn't enough. He tugged another up to his chin.

Of and on he slept. Wind rattled the windows. He dreamed. Words hovered in the dark air. Take nourishment, Zeno said. Travis complained the cruiser wouldn't start. When was Gus going to fix it? I'll keep you warm, a woman said. He couldn't make out her face. She snickered and thinned into the gloom. Somewhere children were chanting boohoo, boohoo, little Gus has the flu.

He awoke, struggled to the bathroom, swallowed aspirin. By Sunday the fever had seeped out of him.

—⁓—

MONDAY. "YOU LOOK LIKE HELL," TRAVIS SAID.

The mug of coffee shook in Gus's hand. "At least I don't hurt anymore," he said.

Travis didn't believe him.

The posters fluttered and went still.

Tuft's Feed and Implement store was almost deserted, the clerks off somewhere eating their lunches.

Wayne Tuft had known Gus in high school. They'd both played basketball, Wayne, a bit over six feet, the center. He wore a red flannel shirt, jeans, and cowboy boots. Gus remembered he'd talked about moving to Texas after graduation, but he joined the army and returned to Harr County after the war.

"You considering raising livestock in your retirement?" Wayne asked.

"It's an idea," Gus said.

"Your compadre over in King County raises beef cattle, Black Angus. You and him friends?"

"Sheriff Pope and I get along."

"Some folks think he only raises cane, but his herd is a nice one. Grows beans and tobacco too. But crops take capital. And they're risky. Tobacco's the safest. And you don't have to like the product, only the cash you carry to the bank."

Gus glanced around. "Billy Hunt here?"

"Not today, only works part-time."

"Good worker?"

"Mostly. He's some moody though."

"Any reason?"

"You stopped him from driving I hear."

"He stopped himself."

"Doubt he sees it that way."

"When he is working, what does he do?"

"Everything from banging around in the implement shop, repairing equipment, to driving the delivery truck. I know I shouldn't, his license being revoked, but I let him do that. He sweeps up when we're done for the day."

"Did he deliver some watering troughs to the Fisk farm?"

"He did, but he wasn't supposed to. The order was written with others on the chalkboard, but it wasn't scheduled to be filled until George Fisk settled his account. My drivers knew George was out of town, and I couldn't sell him as much as a nail until he gave me cash or a good check."

"The hog disease at Mrs. Newsome's place, you knew about that?"

"Sure. Me and my customers have discussed it plenty. Mrs. Newsome did the right thing, destroying the hogs and burning their pen."

"You knew when she planned the burning?"

"She was in to order some special chicken supplement she thinks worthwhile, though I disagree, but I don't want to discourage a paying customer. She said the weather was cooperating and what day she had in mind. She hated to shoot her own hogs. I said I'd do it for her, but she said she was a good shot and felt it was her responsibility."

"I spoke to her on a Tuesday. She told me she'd start the fire next day. When did Billy deliver the troughs?"

"Tuesday. Two weeks tomorrow."

"Do you recall how he got to work that day?"

"Usually on Tuesdays Frieda, our bookkeeper, drives him. They only live about a mile from each other, but that Tuesday Roy brought Billy."

"Do you remember what time Billy left for the Fisks?"

"Truck was loaded and on its way by noon. We delayed a couple of hours because of the road conditions, but we run good tires on all our vehicles. We can go when others can't, or won't."

"Did Billy deliver the troughs by himself?"

"Yeah, they'll bulky, but they're light. Billy's strong enough to handle them without help. He sure took his time though."

"What do you mean?"

"I expected him back by two or two thirty. He showed up at three thirty. Said he'd stopped to help a man change a tire, out-of-state plate, someone passing through, but I suspect he had someone with him—female company, maybe. Or could be he'd met up with Roy and had a beer or two. They do that sometimes. I couldn't smell nothing. Billy's always chewing Juicy Fruit to sweeten his breath."

"May I see the truck?"

"Sure." Wayne led Gus through the implement shop. The truck was parked near the loading dock.

Wayne said, "Stay upwind of that." He pointed to the manure spreader beyond the truck. "Things all seized up. One of Billy's projects. He gets to banging on it to loosen things. I watch him and ask myself why I'm paying a man to whale away on something that's old and not worth fixing. We need to move it before fly season. We're not a storage facility, especially for shit spreaders."

"What's he bang with?"

"Big ol' hammers mostly. Sometimes he'll use a bar of some kind. He gets so frustrated, I think he'd use a rock if he had one."

A speaker broadcast the message that Wayne had a phone call in his office. He shook Gus's hand and told him to take as long as he needed with the truck. No deliveries were scheduled the rest of the day.

There was dried mud on the floor mat on both the driver's side and the passenger's side of the cab, mud mixed with hog waste from the smell of it.

———

BONNIE SAID, "YOU'RE GETTING TO BE such a regular the cook will think we're going steady." The café was empty. "My break time. Let's go outside," she said.

Bonnie lit a cigarette and raised her face to the sun. "I guess the only thing steady about us is your questions. Who is it today?"

"Milly Hicks."

"Her again?"

"You said before the sheriff over there liked her."

"Sheriff Pope showed up. Wanted to see Milly."

"Did she want to see him, or did Miss Harbaugh expect Milly to act like she did?"

A sparrow flew down and pecked at a roll someone had dropped in the grass beyond the parking lot. Bonnie watched the bird and took her time answering.

"A couple of times Milly spent time with Pope away from the hotel." Bonnie leaned against the wall. A car drove in. The sparrow flew away. "Going out of the hotel like that was against Harbaugh's rules, but Pope being who he is, what could she say?"

"Do you think Milly wanted to see Pope outside the hotel?"

"Wasn't physical, if you know what I mean. Wasn't attraction, except on his part. Don't understand her reasons, but she was up to something."

"Any guesses?"

"Steak?"

"*Steak?*"

"Pope had some fancy beef animals. They make good steaks, don't they?"

"They do." The sparrow was back again, pecking at the roll.

"Did Milly ever mention family?"

"I heard her say she had a brother who lived out west. Harbaugh didn't believe her, thought she was making it up and didn't want to tell Harbaugh anything that would identify her in any way."

"You agree?"

"From the window of my room I could see the phone booth across the street. I watched her make a couple of calls, long distance from the amount of coins she'd use, but not a sum you'd need to call to Montana or some state out there. Besides, she'd phone early in the morning and people out west would still be asleep."

"You believe she might have a brother?"

"Might." Bonnie stepped on her cigarette. "Breaks over," she said. She held the door open for Gus. "You coming in?"

"The office needs me," Gus said.

"You just wear me out with questions and dump me, right?"

"My apologies."

"Don't take me serious. Come round anytime, day or night. I enjoy wearing out. I can think of interesting ways to do it."

———

"SBI?" Travis asked.

"I'd call them first. The state DOJ next."

While Travis phoned, Gus went into the cells to check on a young man named Butch, who'd been arrested for stealing ammunition from Spaid's store. Gus asked Butch some questions and told him he'd have to stay overnight.

"I don't like it here," Butch said.

"You get used to it," Gus said.

Travis was off the phone. "The SBI has an agent named Macklin Hicks. I have the number for his regional office."

"Let's try to get him here."

"What should I say?"

"Thank him for the information he gave you before and tell him we'd like to see him again, regarding Sheriff Pope."

"It's late."

"Tomorrow, if possible."

Gus coaxed the cruiser to start. The evening was turning cold. Gus wondered if Rubin would invite him inside or if they would talk in the cruiser, the motor running and the heater blowing cold air.

Gus stopped in the lane and tooted his horn. Rubin could use a dog like Sparky, Gus thought, an animal that wouldn't take kindly to visitors. Rubin opened the door. Gus walked up the stone path Rubin had set down when the weather was warm, flat brown stones he'd carried from the river.

"I know where the woman is. Tell me who she is."

Rubin motioned Gus inside. More books with pictures of plants were open on the table.

"Are you a wine drinker? I have a bottle of Chablis," Rubin said.

"Who delivered that?" Gus asked.

"A benevolent stranger."

"You mean the Canadian who passes through dry counties selling spirits?"

"A spiritualist then. He offers wine too."

"Harr County isn't completely dry."

"Yes, but the available vintages are hardly worth drinking. The Chablis will be excellent."

"I'd like a taste," Gus said. He stood until Rubin uncorked the bottle, handed Gus his glass, and invited him to sit down.

"You first," Rubin said.

"The woman is safe. She's well-cared for. She's living comfortably. She even has a new bicycle."

"Where?"

"In the county." Gus sipped his Chablis. "This is very good." He raised his glass to Rubin. "Now it's your turn," he said.

"Her name is Marie Kessler. Her father was Otto Kessler, a Jew. Her mother, Christina, was not. Otto was wealthy. He kept his fine collection at his estate outside of Paris. Marie was a lovely young woman, stunning, but difficult. Now she is neither." Rubin swirled his glass. "Where is she?"

"At Twelve Trees."

"The best house in the county. I'm sure Mr. Levoy is treating her well."

"I believe she is looking after Teddy, his grandson."

"The damaged one. Two damaged people."

"Was Marie always mute?"

"No." Rubin nodded toward the window. "Dark now. It should be dark. Her story is dark and complicated." He sipped his wine. "She grew up beautiful and spoiled. She loved showing off. She loved exposing herself to men who could not have her. She loved creating an expectation she would never fulfill."

Rubin paused, remembering. He smiled sadly. "Her father commissioned her portrait. A young painter named Shüle, a German living in Paris. He fell under Marie's spell. He made two portraits, the one her father saw and approved, and the one he did not, the one Shüle painted from memory. In the official portrait she wears a dress Chanel created for her. The emeralds in her necklace match the color of her eyes. In the other portrait she wears nothing."

Rubin set his glass on the table and looked around the room. "I am trying to recall the poet, one of your early English ones, what he wrote about such a woman. 'Noli me tangere, For I am Caesar's I am.' You studied literature. What's the rest of it?"

"'And wild for to hold, though I seem tame.'"

"Exactly. And who was the poet?"

"Thomas Wyatt."

"Ah yes. Not Goethe, not Rilke, but interesting. Marie was impossible to tame." Rubin took a deeper sip of wine and disappeared into his own thoughts.

"Marie?" Gus said.

"Yes, I realize you're not here to pass the evening with my memories. All right then. The Germans swept through the Low Countries. Before they reached Paris, Otto sent Madame Kessler to England. He remained because he loved his art. Marie believed her body would save her. The Germans soon showed her how wrong she was. After they used her, they let her leave. She said she had relatives in Montreal. That wasn't true, but it was what Kessler had told her to tell them. They arranged her travel—the slow scenic route by way of South America. Otto's estate appealed to the Germans, as he knew it would. He was a Jew, but they allowed him to leave as well. Why not Montreal since he had family there? Perhaps he and his daughter would be reunited.

Rubin paused to drink his wine. "In the meantime the Germans who occupied Otto's estate discovered that two of the works they coveted, a Hals and a Holbein, were fakes. Otto was beyond their reach, Marie was not. The German agents caught up her with in Rio. Someone had advised them that Marie knew where the real paintings were and how to get them. She could tell them nothing. A tongue is an obstinate organ to remove, but they tried. Perhaps her body did save her. They finally gave up. Surely they had noticed the cheap bracelet she wore, but they didn't pay it much attention. Ce n'est pas aussi simple que cela paraît."

Rubin emptied his glass. "There's more than meets the eye, you would say. The plastic on the outside hid a tiny metal plate underneath etched with numbers to a Geneva account where Kessler planned to send his most valuable art for safekeeping. Kessler and I discussed whether he should tell Marie how important the bracelet was, how she should guard it. He decided not to tell her about the numbers. He believed she would treasure it because he had given it to her. They were very close."

Rubin spoke softly now as if to himself. "*Das trauma...*" He looked at Gus. "The trauma, she has never spoken again."

Gus thought he heard a car. He stood and drew back the curtain. The road was dark and empty.

"So," Rubin continued, "Marie finally arrived in Montreal. Of course she didn't know where to find Kessler. She asked the police. They told her he had been murdered. People at the embassy had arranged for his burial. They handed over the few possessions he had, which included his suit. A Nazi would have cut it open looking for gold or diamonds, but the police had simply folded the suit and laid it in a box. Marie found the emerald necklace in the lining."

Rubin got up, refilled their glasses, and sat down again. He swirled his glass and sipped. "Such wonderful acidity," he said. "All that limestone."

"You told her about the numbers, didn't you?" Gus said.

"Yes." Rubin laughed. "Now, in the end, they're not so important anymore."

"And the necklace?"

Marie took it and dropped out of sight. She worked here and there. When she tired of one town or city, she moved to another. No one suspected she owned valuable jewelry."

"What about her mother?"

"A German bomb fell on Madame Kessler's flat. She had been warned but refused to leave. As for the Hals and the Holbein, Kessler believed the fakes would fool the Germans for a while. Just before Sylvester died, Tony overheard Kessler telling Sylvester about sending the real ones along with Marie's portrait to Geneva and how Marie would know how to retrieve them, but that's what Kessler wanted him to think. He never really trusted anyone, even my father. Kessler sent the real ones to England with his wife. The bomb destroyed them as well, but only my friend and I, and now you, know that."

Rubin savored more wine. "Can you see the picture I'm painting for you?"

"Rubin, it's the artist I'm interested in."

"Sheriff, I've committed all my crimes years ago and quite far from your jurisdiction."

"You're the forger."

"Copier, to be exact. I don't have the skill of a forger. I did a favor for Otto."

"What are you doing now?"

"Enjoying a lovely wine and talking to you."

"You're still doing favors for Otto."

"I'm still in love with his daughter."

Both men were silent. A clock ticked. Gus went to the window again. Nothing but the dark, empty road again.

"You were following her," he said.

"My friend was, the one I said drove me. He thought he had located Marie in Virginia. When she left there and came here, he told me he was certain. He would prefer I not reveal his name. He's a retired policeman. Otto's murder was one of his cases."

"Whose idea was it to use the necklace as bait?"

"His. For years he has suspected not only did Tony Crim kill Kessler but also Tony believed Marie, if he could find her, would lead him to the Hals and Holbein. My friend knows Tony's habits, what he reads for example, and putting the necklace in the catalog was a way to lure Tony into the open."

Gus leaned against the wall. The cold outside seeped around the window and chilled his neck. "What now?" he asked.

"Surely Tony is about to leave."

"With your friend behind him?"

"Indeed. And you are left with your own crime to solve."

"And a long night to think about it," Gus said.

———

TUESDAY MORNING TRAVIS PATROLLED WHILE GUS stayed in the office waiting for Macklin Hicks.

"Call me Mack," he said and shook Gus's hand. In his forties, he was slight and stooped, his hair turned white, and he wore glasses—a man who wouldn't stand out in a crowd. Gus thought he looked more like a professor than an investigator.

"We're sorry about your sister," Gus said.

He offered Mack Travis's chair because it was more comfortable than the other and poured Mack a cup of coffee.

"She…" Mack shook his head.

"You've been here before, haven't you? You gave my deputy your sister's dental records, but you didn't give him your name."

"Milly was finding things out, but I didn't want people to find out about her. We talked on the phone. We didn't meet face-to-face anymore."

"Was she working for you?"

"Not officially. It came about by accident. Milly studied sociology in college. She was interested in how different people live and get along, or don't. She'd do various kinds of jobs and take notes about the people she met. In the course of getting to know—what should I call them, ladies?—the women at the hotel, she figured out that Sheriff Pope was spending a lot more than he could afford on a sheriff's salary. To put it politely, he took a shine to her and she went along with it. Whatever she found out, she told me."

"What did she find out?"

"Pope's involved in the usual rural crimes—illegal liquor, selling favors, like influencing who won paving contracts, and getting paid to settle grievances with unexplained mishaps. Lots of small fires in King County. He also receives payoffs from Harbaugh and the Crown Club and a gas station or two that have slot machines or other gambling devices."

Mack hunched over and stared at his feet. He brushed some dirt from the cuff of his trousers. "I need to arrange to take Milly's remains back to Raleigh for burial. Word will get around. I know you don't want that."

"Give me two days," Gus said.

"All right," Mack said.

The wanted posters fluttered and went still. Gus left Travis a note, saying he had an errand to run in Kingsville.

Miss Jean's wasn't busy. Two women were sitting under the dryers, flipping through magazines. Brenda leaned against the wall, filing her nails. Miss Jean gave Gus a puzzled look. "Just wanted to make sure Brenda is all right," Gus said.

Brenda said she was and thanked Gus for asking about her.

The sky was blue and clear, a Southern breeze. Maybe winter wouldn't last forever. Gans's shop was nearby. The display of silver dollars in the window caught Gus's attention. So did the medal.

Mr. Gans was polishing silverware. He held up a soup spoon for Gus's approval. "Lovely service," he said. "If there were a Mrs. Salt, she'd appreciate it."

Gus looked at the other pieces in the velvet compartments in a mahogany box. "Mrs. Salt's initial wouldn't be A.D. She might not like that."

"Anything I can show you?"

"The medal in the window."

"Ah, the Lucky Lindy." Gans fetched it and laid it in Gus's palm: Lindbergh on one side and the date 1957; his plane on the other and the date 1927.

"How much?" Gus asked.

"Twenty dollars. Would be worth twice that if someone hadn't drilled a tiny hole for a chain."

"When did you acquire it?"

"That roughneck who works at the hotel brought it in."

"Roy Hunt?"

"I believe so. He wanted thirty dollars. Fifteen is what I told the lady before."

"What lady?"

"One that was here the middle of December. She said a friend of hers had given her the medal and she wanted to know how much it was worth so that she could return the favor and give her friend something of equal value, a Christmas present."

"So you'd seen the medal before?"

"Yes, but I didn't tell the man that."

"I don't suppose the lady told you her name."

"She saw a pearl brooch her friend might like. I said it was worth forty, but I'd sell it for twenty-five. The lady wrote me a check and signed it Millicent Hicks. She didn't have a driver's license, so I couldn't verify her name, but the check cashed."

"Had she ever been in the shop before?"

"No, but I'd seen her at the cafeteria on Long Street. Folks from the hotel often eat there. I had the impression she might have been one of Miss Harbaugh's flock. Mind you, I don't seek Miss Harbaugh's services, but I've heard men comment on how fastidious she is about the way her ladies appear when callers arrive. Yet when you see one of ladies away from the hotel, they dress in jeans and cheap shirts and never wear makeup. Miss Hicks had on a pair of coveralls. I guess they're roomy and comfortable. Not feminine, though."

Gus took out his billfold and handed Gans twenty dollars. He wrapped the medal in paper and gave it to Gus.

Gans walked Gus to the door and followed him outside. "After such grim weather, it feels almost balmy. I'm tempted to take a walk," Gans said.

"Good idea," Gus said.

The flags on the Johnson House porch fluttered in the breeze. Mr. Coombs mentioned the Groundhog Day champagne evening. Never too early to make a reservation.

Gus said he wanted to see the basement.

Mr. Coombs pointed to the cot near the boiler. "I moved it. Someone put it back."

"Moved it when?"

"Weeks ago."

"Betty liked it where it is, didn't she?"

"She could have been staying here again. I never did get her key."

Gus drove across the bridge and parked on the Harr County side of the river. He retrieved his boots from the trunk, put them on, and skidded down the embankment. At least in winter there wasn't as much trash as there would be in summer. He found a long stick and poked at a few cans and bottles and soggy cardboard. He kept walking. The duffel was caught in a cove of cattails. He should have found it before.

This time the old cruiser wouldn't start. Gus radioed Travis to send Buster Green with his tow truck. While Gus waited, he unzipped the duffel bag: socks, jeans, coveralls, underwear, a couple of sweaters, a wool coat, a pair of Keds. The Minox camera was wrapped in plastic looped by rubber bands. There was a soggy copy of *The Mind of the South*. He thumbed the pages and found the note: *Chère Milly, the brooch look nice on me. Marie.*

Buster arrived. The sky was turning dark. The wind off the water was cold now. Gus watched Buster fuss with the tow chain and raise the cruiser's front wheels off the ground. He moved the pile of hunting magazines off the passenger seat and made a place for Gus to sit.

Four thirty, the county garage was still open. Buster parked behind the building and eased the car down. "New one's inside." he said. "Real pretty. Shiny black paint, gold letters. You'll be king of the road."

Gus didn't have time to look. He walked to the courthouse and up the stairs to his uncle's office. Ora Green was tidying her desk, preparing to leave. "Poetry group tonight," she said.

Abe came out of his office. Gus explained he needed to borrow Abe's car.

Abe explained his car was unavailable. He was driving to Burlington for supper.

"Another thing," Abe said. "The county isn't going to repair your cruiser anymore. It's ancient and it's been your personal property for months. The county should never have let you use it. We could have borrowed one from the state motor pool. That was my fault."

"If the new one's ready, tonight I'll take it."

"Can't. We're still checking it out. The paperwork isn't complete." Abe ran his hand over his bald head. "Is what you need it for official?"

Gus shook his head.

"Be yours Thursday," Abe said.

Gus walked back to the station. A few flakes of snow spun out of the dark sky. Duncan was filling his thermos.

"Heard about the old cruiser," he said. "Oh, Mrs. Wooten called you. She's going to be at the diner"—Duncan looked at his watch—"in ten minutes."

Gus said, "Give me time to eat at Bowen's, then drive me to Dazzle's place. Pick me up there by nine and take me home. Travis will bring me in tomorrow."

——⟋⟍⟋⟍——

Neva sat at a table in the corner. The diner was always crowded from noon until two. It was almost empty now.

Marla had gone home, and Wally Bowen waited on customers himself.

"What do you recommend?" Neva asked.

"How hungry are you?"

"Not very. I'm really here for your company."

"I heard your painter has gone."

"He asked me to go with him, but...I don't know...I couldn't."

"Couldn't leave Zeno?"

"He's a habit, I guess. Like smoking. I tried to quit that once."

"And love has nothing to do with it?"

Neva stared down at the menu. "Gus, I don't know." She turned the menu over. "Maybe, but in the end Tony left me. I always sensed he wasn't a patient man. Something was always on his mind, and it wasn't me."

When she looked up, Wally was standing there. "Round steak is good tonight. Served with mashed potatoes."

"Soup?" Neva asked.

"Beef barley."

"Soup is enough for me," she said.

"Meatloaf," Gus said and handed the menus to Wally.

Neva opened her purse and took out her cigarettes. "Like I said, I tried to quit once."

"Neva, your painter may have been involved in something you don't want to know about."

Neva held the cigarette without lighting it. "Are you going to tell me anyway?"

"It's not my story to tell."

"Whose story is it?"

"Rubin Dazzle's."

"And he's told it to you and you can't repeat it?"

"He's told me some of it. I'm going to see him tonight."

Wally brought Neva's soup and a plate of crackers. "Meatloaf be right out," he said.

"Don't wait for me," Gus said.

Neva put down her cigarette, picked up her spoon, and began to eat. "Tasty," she said.

Wally reappeared. "Plate's hot." He set down Gus's meal.

"Wally," Neva asked, "does it ever bother you to see the same faces day in and day out?"

"It would bother me if I didn't. Regular customers keep me in business."

"But the same faces, the same orders, the same stories. The same, the same, the same…?"

"I see it different," Wally said. "People change, they retire, they get old, they die. Sometimes it breaks my heart."

Neva watched him walk back to the kitchen. "Tony didn't break my heart," she said. "When something's too good to last, it won't. I figured he would leave. I was never sure why he was here in the first place."

"That's part of the story Mr. Dazzle can tell you."

Neva finished her soup, lit her cigarette, and walked around the diner, examining the faded photographs of Harr County that Wally had framed and hung on the walls.

Neva sat down again. "There a picture of Twelve Trees taken the year you were born."

"I know," Gus said.

"Have you spent much time with Percy since he married again?"

"Not much."

"Is he happy?"

"Don't know."

"I wonder how Ruth likes it there—Percy always talking about the past, or thinking about it anyway, and she probably trying not to think about it. Any idea?"

Gus pushed his plate aside. "I didn't see Ruth the last time I visited."

Neva's eyes widened. "Maybe he's locked her away from the world, or even done away with her. If I were a writer, I'd set a Gothic tale there." Neva stubbed out her cigarette. "But you were going to be the writer, weren't you?"

"A long time ago."

"What about Blossom, did you ever finish reading her book?"

"Mostly."

Neva reached across the table and pressed Gus's hands between hers. "Love. Love has a lot to do with it, with me and Zeno, and with you and Blossom. I need to do something. So do you."

Gus saw Duncan stop outside. He stood up and took out his wallet,

"No, I'm paying," Neva said. "Then I'm going home. I'll light a fire in the fireplace, change into some glorious silk pajamas, open a bottle of Zeno's favorite sipping whiskey, and pretend a bunch of stuff never happened."

Gus followed Neva into the night. She stopped and reached for his hand again. "It would break my heart if Zeno died. And it would break my heart if you did."

—◊◊◊—

DUNCAN TURNED ON THE WIPERS. "About a quarter-inch so far," he said. "An inch or more predicted by morning. Only seen four or five cars."

"People staying home, being sensible," Gus said.

"What about you?"

"Rubin serves good wine. I enjoy his company. He helps me understand things, make sense of things."

"The way you've laid it out to Travis, you've made sense of what happened in the hog pen."

"What did he tell you?"

"Either Roy or Billy Hunt struck Milly Hicks, split her skull, and concealed her body in Mrs. Newsome's hog pen the day before they knew she was going to burn it down. They probably used a hammer from Billy's work and they carried the body in the truck Billy drove to make a delivery at the Fisk farm."

The cruiser skidded when Duncan turned onto Girty Road. Nights like this, a Jeep would come in handy. He looked down the road, but he couldn't see clearly enough to know if Piney was out in his.

"I'm not sure it's what was intended," Gus said. "Women make Billy nervous. Milly taunted him for it—made fun of him. Roy took it personal too. The brothers wanted to teach Milly a lesson. She was on her way to Rubin's. They caught up with her. There was a scuffle. I'm sure they took her somewhere else. Roy has a temper, especially when it comes to women."

"Took her where, you think?"

"I'll get a warrant to search their property."

"I thought you usually just went and did it."

"Abe's warned me."

Duncan stopped in Rubin's lane. Gus got out. Duncan waited until he saw the trailer door open and Gus step inside before backing down to the road. For an instant the headlights flashed across the distant trees. No sign of a Jeep.

—◦◦◦◦—

"I EXPECTED YOU." Rubin poured and handed Gus his glass. "This bottle won't be as good as the one I served before." The men sat down. "What's your question?

"Do you believe in coincidence?"

"Things happen we can't explain any other way."

"What about the towel?"

"Marie liked to sew and knit. The towel was just a towel with a figure on it. I guessed Tony would read what the reporter wrote about it, the figure digging a hole. When the towel disappeared, I assumed Tony stole it. I assumed he would interpret an innocent scene as something that referred to his obsession, the bracelet. So I planted the bracelet for him to find." Rubin smiled. "And now he's off to discover there's no Hals, no Holbein."

"Who helped you?"

"Mrs. Newsome."

"How much?"

"She didn't take money."

"What then?"

"I promised her I'd buy her supper at the Johnson House. She's never been there. She's never ridden in a taxi before either."

Gus took the medal out of his pocket. "Give her this."

Rubin unwrapped the paper. "Lindbergh was quite handsome. A bit of a fascist though," he said.

"How did you come by the bracelet?"

"I'm sure Tony killed Marie's father. I believe he would have killed Marie for it. I cautioned her. Keep in mind she had not met Tony, but I had described him to her. Near the end of the year she was passing the bank and saw him. He didn't

see her, but she must have decided then to stay out of sight.
I found her green bag with the bracelet inside it on my steps
New Year's morning."

"She rode here on her bicycle?"

"Yes, you were wrong about that. She left it here. That's
what concerned me. I thought someone might have—*napped*?
What is the word?—kidnapped her. But then why wouldn't
they take the bag too?"

"Rubin, why didn't you explain all this to me before?"

"Because I was ashamed."

"You weren't here, were you?"

"No. I was elsewhere."

"Would you care to tell me a name?"

"Lloyd."

"Mr., Mrs., Miss?"

"Miss."

Gus took a long drink and stared into the distance.

"What are you thinking?" Rubin asked.

"Marie must have thought it was safer to walk across the
fields and through the woods than ride alone on the road."

"So much pain. So much pain. The old days you forget for
a while, then a sound, a smell, even a silent bird on a winter
branch reminds you. Marie was right to be afraid. You asked
me if I own a weapon. I do not. How could I have protected
her? With words?"

"She was a friend of Milly Hicks."

"Yes, Milly looked out for her."

"And Milly was trying to get here when she disappeared."

"I had promised to lend her money for her kindness to
Marie. She was going away. She hadn't decided where."

"Did she tell you why?"

"She said she wanted to go away and write about some things she found out."

"What things, did she tell you?"

Rubin shook his head.

Gus stood up and buttoned his jacket. "When your trees need planting, I'll be ready to help."

———

PINEY WAS THINKING HOW SNOW KEPT people off the roads, tucked away in their warm beds, but not him.

Eight o'clock, dark as midnight. The only light visible in the landscape was the window of the trailer. Piney slowed and stopped. He rolled down his window and rested his rifle on the door. What was the Jew doing? Reading books in their queer alphabet? Drinking their sweet disgusting wine? Counting money? Shekels did they call it? Piney waited.

Behind the curtain the outline of a man appeared, all gauzy and dreamlike. Piney fired and drove away. More snow and hours before daylight, he thought, and even more time before anyone noticed a broken window and pounded on the trailer door to find out if Dazzle was all right. He didn't have friends, except maybe the sheriff, and he didn't patrol much on Girty Road. Any more snow and he might not patrol at all until the sun melted it into that gritty slush Piney disliked so much.

At home Piney took off his coat and boots and laid the rifle on the kitchen table. He filled a tall glass with clear whiskey and sat down with a bottle of solvent and patches to clean the gun. Drinking came first though. He emptied his glass and poured himself another and sipped most of it.

He felt drowsy. He leaned across the table and rested his

head on his arm. His body floated away. He was standing deep in snow. He could taste it: cold and sharp with a hint of iron, like when you cut yourself and taste your blood. He opened his eyes.

"We'll need your rifle," Gus said.

Piney stared. The other deputy—Piney couldn't remember his name—was standing beside the sheriff. Piney reached for his glass.

"You've had enough for tonight," Gus said.

"Some for you." Piney pointed to the whiskey jar. "And your deputy."

"I'll just sit a minute," Gus said. He handed the rifle to Duncan to take to the cruiser. He told Duncan to keep the motor on, and the heater.

"You missed two people, me and Mr. Dazzle. You ought to be thankful."

"I suppose you're sure it was me."

"Duncan saw you drive away. Your Jeep leaves clear tracks to follow."

"Not much to talk about then, is there?"

"Let's discuss the other nights you've been parked off the road watching the trailer. See anything I would want to know?"

"Is this like one of those quiz shows? If I give the right answer, I sleep in my own bed tonight?"

"You have the right answer?"

"I saw Roy Hunt pull a woman out of a car."

"By himself?"

"His brother was with him, driving that flathead Mercury they got off one of their relatives. The woman was in a little car. Something must have happened to it. Didn't want to go."

"Did she put up a fight?"

"Oh yes. They tussled right much. Rolled around in the weeds. Roy was punching her and yanking at something around her neck and she went all limp. Then he and Billy dragged her to the road and shoved her into the Mercury. Roy got in to drive and waited for Billy to get a bag out of her car."

"Do you recall when this happened?"

"Sunday night."

Gus picked up the whiskey jar and shook it. "Lots of little bubbles."

"Means it's good. How was my answer?"

"I'll keep the rifle. Hunting season's over. And you know you shouldn't be shooting in the dark." Gus smelled the whiskey and sighed.

"You don't want me or one of my deputies to ever see you near Girty Road again. And keep clear of Mr. Dazzle. Don't call him or mail him or threaten him in any way. Even if I'm not sheriff anymore, things can happen you don't want to happen." Gus handed Piney his glass. "You might as well finish it," he said. "Make you sleep better."

"I'll do like you say, Sheriff. I surely will."

ANOTHER FROSTY MORNING. Travis drove. Gus stared at the brown fields and bare trees, holding the warrant in his hand.

"After we're through we can warm up with coffee at the cafe in Ruffin," Gus said.

"Just looking at Bonnie can warm a person plenty," Travis said.

Hunt was carelessly painted on the mailbox on the bent

pole beside the bush along the roadside. Travis parked in the rutted grass in front of the trailer, a rusted Airstream resting on blocks. Gus broke the lock and opened the door.

"Deserted like it is, we didn't need a warrant," Travis said.

Empty beer bottles and paper plates with dried smears of spaghetti covered the table between two chairs, which faced a milking stool where there might have been a portable TV. The bent coat hanger might have improved reception.

A skillet with congealed grease and a pot with crusted tomato sauce filled the kitchen sink. A bottle of spoiled milk in the refrigerator, one small enough for a person to pick up and carry off. A dead roach lay on its back beside a crust of bread. "Need some fresh air in here," Gus said. "The place stinks."

There was a cot and a sleeping bag. No clothes. A towel, some rags. Three *Playboy* centerfolds taped to the wall. A sliver of soap. A used razorblade. Urine in the toilet bowl. Another dead roach in the corner, a live one scuttling around the washstand rimmed with stained linoleum.

The door to the shed near the row of gum trees behind the trailer was open. The floor had been swept clean. The smell of bleach hung the air.

The oil drum used for a burn barrel was cold. Travis helped Gus tip it over. They picked through the ashes and found bits of a charred shirt, part of a pair of overalls, most of two shoes too small to fit either Roy or Billy, even a scorched bra.

Travis said, "Wouldn't you think if you wanted to burn stuff up, you'd keep at it until the fire did its work?"

"Folks can be careless," Gus said. "He knelt down and sifted through more ashes. "Or maybe not," he said so softly Travis could hardly hear him.

———ᗯᗯᗯ———

BONNIE SMILED AT GUS. "Brought your sidekick this time." She winked at Travis. "I know what the sheriff wants. What about you, sidekick?"

"Coffee, same as him," Travis said.

"Just made a fresh pot."

Travis watched her walk away. Gus had gone to the restroom to wash his hands.

Bonnie returned and poured two cups. She set the sugar bowl beside Gus's. "I know he likes it sweet," she said.

Gus came back and sat down. Bonnie leaned over the counter and sniffed his sleeve. "You can wash up, but that smoke smell gets in your clothes."

"You have any particular smoke smell in mind?" Gus asked.

"I do, and I bet you do too."

"Tell me," Gus said.

"You been nosing around that trailer the Hunt boys rent."

"You want to say more?"

"I can do better than that." She looked around the room. A couple in the corner were waiting for their check. She took it over and cleared their table. The man paid and she brought him change.

She filled Gus and Travis's cups again. "Sheriff Pope was here, sitting in a booth talking to Mr. Timms, my boss. He owns the trailer where the Hunts stayed. Pope smelled like he was smoke himself."

"When?" Gus asked.

"Sheriff, I never pay much attention to the calendar, but it was just after the Hunts gave notice and left the county. Mr. Timms and Pope are friends. From what I overheard, Timms asked Pope to check out the property because he was concerned they might have done something to the trailer. Timms is like that—always suspicious."

Another couple came in and Bonnie took them menus. She sent their order to the kitchen before she returned to the counter. "It was late in the afternoon, I remember that. When I got off, I went over there myself."

"You mean to the trailer?"

"Yes. That barrel out back was still warm but wasn't any fire left. Looked like someone had damped it down with water or something. I pulled out the remains of a pair of smoldering jeans. They're still in my car." Bonnie took the keys from her pocket and handed them to Gus. "Behind the building. Brown Ford. In the trunk."

The car was parked near a stunted magnolia. Gus opened the trunk. What remained of the jeans lay across the spare tire. Gus used his jack handle to spread the waistband.

"Thirty-eight or forty," Gus said. "Too big for the Hunts, too big for Hicks. About right for Pope."

Gus went back inside, gave Bonnie her keys, and asked what time she finished work. Five, she said and reminded him where she lived. It usually took her a few minutes to get out of her uniform.

On the way back to Levoy, Gus asked Travis to stop at Zeno's clinic.

"You need medical attention?" Travis asked.

"I need information," Gus said, "if Zeno will give me any."

———

ANOTHER COLD NIGHT. Bonnie opened the door. "Took your time getting here," she said.

She wore slacks and a flannel shirt, several buttons undone, nothing underneath as far as Gus could see.

In the kitchen Bonnie opened two beers. Gus took the bottle she handed him. "How well do you know Sheriff Pope?" he asked.

"How well do you think I know him?"

"He got you pregnant."

"Who told you that?"

Gus looked past Bonnie's shoulder at the calendar on the wall. January was decorated with a bright red cardinal perched on a snowy branch. "Zeno Wooton."

"I'm surprised he told you."

"He didn't, just ignored me. He does that when I'm right. When I'm wrong, he says I'm wrong. I didn't tell him the rest."

"Tell me."

"Pope smelled like smoke. You guessed where he'd been. You went there and pulled out what was left of a pair of jeans. From the waist size I figure they would fit Pope. There were other clothes burned too, including a pair of shoes that would fit a woman."

Bonnie drank her beer and studied Gus. "You're saying the britches I pulled out of the barrel are Pope's?"

"Yes."

"I don't understand."

"I didn't either, at first."

"Now what are you thinking?"

"You have Pope's burned jeans in your car. Why? He got you pregnant and you're not friendly with him anymore. The jeans are evidence of something to bring up against him."

"Evidence of what?"

"I'll work backward. Why were the Hunts burning clothes

at all? I know they kidnapped Milly Hicks. If the Hunts were burning anything they wore that might have her blood on them, like the pair of boots that hardly burned at all, there's a problem."

"Sheriff, now I'm really lost. What problem?"

"How much the fire didn't burn. The boots and the women's shoes for example. There was even part of a bra. The fire didn't destroy evidence, it created evidence."

"The Hunts aren't geniuses."

"They're not stupid either."

"So?"

"They didn't start the fire."

"Who did?"

"Pope. He let it burn just enough for me to find what Hicks wore and conclude the Hunts killed her."

Bonnie stared at Gus, tapping the lip of the bottle against her chin. "You're saying Pope is making it seem like the Hunts were destroying evidence and what he's doing is pointing his finger at them, making them look guilty of killing Hicks?"

"What's wrong with my theory?"

"Why would Pope mix his clothes with theirs?"

"He didn't."

"Who did?"

"Someone who had a reason not to care for him. Someone who might have something he wore. Someone who burned it to make it look like it was in a fire. Someone—"

"Like me?"

"Am I wrong?"

"How much trouble am I in?"

"You provided helpful information about the barrel and what was in it. What you did with the jeans pointed me to

Pope, and I'm sure he's guilty. A sheriff needs help from the community to do his job. A good lawyer will tell you that."

Bonnie followed Gus to the door. They stood looking out at the dark. She said, "When I told Pope I was pregnant, he threw me on the ground. Then he kicked me. Then he kicked me again. Then I wasn't pregnant anymore."

She started to turn away, but Gus held her. After a while she wiped her eyes.

"When Zeno introduced us, he called you Bonnie L. What's the L stand for?"

"Lloyd," Bonnie said.

"I thought it might," Gus said. He was also sure she had delivered the poems in the night, but it wasn't important anymore, and he didn't ask.

———

THURSDAY AFTERNOON. Gus had left Travis in charge. Percy had come outside to admire the new cruiser. Gus followed him into the house.

"Ruth's got herself a dog," Percy said.

In the library a shaggy setter lay on the Persian carpet by the desk. "Meet Snaf, short for snafu, which, I believe, is an acronym for a vulgar expression common in the military."

Snaf raised its head, eyed Gus, and settled down again.

"Not the most energetic animal, but Ruth likes him. Problem is, the dog prefers downstairs and Ruth has converted the old sewing room upstairs into her special space. She doesn't see much of the critter."

"What about you, are you seeing much of Ruth?"

"Gus, I require neither instruction nor advice from you

about how to carry on with my bride. I already get plenty from Mrs. Ravenel." Percy pointed to a chair. Embers glowed in the fireplace. "If you're staying, I'll lay on more wood."

"I have a couple of questions."

"Only two?" Percy lifted a decanter from the silver tray on the table under the tall window.

"Nothing for me," Gus said.

"Only thirsty for answers?"

"One way to put it."

Percy filled his glass and sat down in the chair opposite Gus. "Two weeks since that body was found. You here to tie up loose ends?"

"Teddy's new caretaker is the mute woman people thought was the victim in the hog pen."

"I never denied it."

"You called her Alice."

"Seemed a good idea at the time."

"A better idea would have been for you to tell me about her."

"She showed up at my door. She wrote her name for me and wrote she needed help. I trusted her, and I trusted you to figure things out."

"How's she's get along with Teddy?"

"Real well. They've developed their own language, all signs and gestures. She can take him anywhere. I've never seen him so calm." Snaf roused himself and eased down again beside Percy. He stroked the dog's ear. "Could be they're in love."

"And what would come to that?"

"Gus, don't be cynical."

"You're right." He reached into his jacket and took out the letter. He leaned forward and handed it to Percy.

"You need your glasses?"

"Not necessary," Percy said.

"What do you think is necessary?"

"That we sit here by the fire, like family." Percy read the letter. "You suspected, didn't you?"

"A few years ago I found my father's service record tucked away in some garage invoices I'd never paid attention to. I was born in November 1919, almost exactly a year after the armistice. The army kept him in Europe until February dismantling equipment to ship back to the states. Then he waited for transport. He didn't see my mother again until the middle of March."

"Were you ever going to say anything?"

"You hadn't. Why should I?"

"Because Teddy is incompetent and you have a valid claim to Twelve Trees."

"It's Ruth's claim now."

"Do you think she wants it?"

"I have no idea."

"When I die, she might stay on for a while, but she has no abiding interest in Twelve Trees." Percy shrugged. "Of course I hoped she would. I was planning for Twelve Trees and Teddy." Percy tasted his drink and smiled. "You know, when the Union boys occupied Kingsville, their commander, a major named Evans, had in mind crossing the river and burning Twelve Trees, but he was tired, I guess, or merely lazy, and decided the comforts of a clean bed at Johnson's Inn, as it was called then, tasty meals, decent drink, and probably the company of an indecent woman were better than torching the home of some local Confederate. "But"—Percy savored more whiskey—"sometimes I think he might have done me a favor if he had burned the place. What's your opinion?"

"You're tired and disappointed the future isn't as clear as you want it to be."

"Gus, help me out. Twelve Trees is yours, if you want it. I've told you that before."

"Tell me about you and Nellie, you and my mother."

"She'd driven over from Psalter Forge a couple of times to look for a property Jeremiah could use for his repair shop when he was out of service. Nellie and Jeremiah weren't married yet. Nellie was quite lovely. I saw her walking on Main Street, sightseeing the big houses, the Adgers' place and the old Wooten homeplace. I introduced myself. And…well…"

"Percy, let me save you the trouble of concocting a story you want me to believe. You may have met Nellie and admired her, but you didn't seduce her. She always spoke of you with respect and gratitude, but not the way she would have if you were my father. I assumed she was grateful to you for a favor you'd done her. The livery stable Jeremiah converted to his garage cost more to buy than they had to spend, and you helped out. But there must be something else that has to do with me. It's time I know what it is."

Snaf had stretched out near Percy's feet, his body quivering in a doggie dream. Percy stared down at his empty glass. "The man had been discharged and bought himself a car with his pay. He was driving south. The winter was warm that year. We had daffodils up by Valentine's Day. The man was drinking and joyriding. He came upon Nellie. She had driven out to see Twelve Trees. She had stopped the car and was walking, enjoying a bright afternoon. That's when the man saw her."

Percy took a deep breath and raised his head.

"As I said, Nellie was a lovely woman, but he didn't treat

her that way. I was driving home from town and found her sitting on the roadside, dazed and dirty. She stayed at Twelve Trees for a while. Doctor Wilson tended her. The old sheriff found the man's car, but he couldn't find the man. I offered a reward, a thousand dollars, but it didn't do any good."

"Was anyone ever going to tell me?"

"Only five of us knew the truth. It was Nellie's decision. You were born wanted and healthy, so she never said. Now they're all gone, except me."

Percy picked up the note. "What I wrote refers to the reward money. I opened an account. The thousand dollars has grown some. It's all yours. I put off telling you for one reason or another. Now I was waiting for you to retire."

Gus stood up and took the empty glass out of Percy's hand. "Nellie was a good mother," he said. "Jeremiah was good too."

"He died too young. I'll die too old," Percy said.

Gus brought Percy a full glass. "Don't be in a hurry."

"What about the Hunt brothers?" Percy said. "I understand the troopers in South Carolina found them. What are they charged with?"

"First-degree kidnapping and accessory to murder to start with."

"But they didn't kill Hicks?"

"Their idea of scaring her to make her stop taunting Billy was to kidnap her and hold her in the shed behind their trailer. But it was Pope who killed her because she could provide proof of his corruption. Not sure what Pope had on the brothers, but he convinced them to get rid of the body. When they moved away, he tried to frame them. It should have worked."

"They'll testify against Pope?"

"That's the deal."

"Where is Pope?"

"Running."

Percy sighed and took a deep drink. "You filled out the law school application?"

"I'm thinking about it."

"Think about Twelve Trees too. Blossom likes it here."

"She likes California."

"California doesn't have seasons like we do. It's always summer there."

"California has mountains and snow."

"Lots of poetry about snow."

"Winter gets in the mind. Sometimes words are the only way to make it go away," Gus said.

"Used to be I could recite that Frost poem 'Stopping by Woods on a Snowy Evening.' Can't anymore, only a few lines left in my head—'The woods are lovely, dark and deep, But I have promises to keep, And miles to go before I sleep.' Thing is, I have too many promises but not enough miles left in me."

"You have a few," Gus said.

"Enjoy 'em while I can, I guess."

"I guess," Gus said and let himself out.

A woman stood beside Teddy pointing to the sky, the clouds furling and unfurling. When she heard the door close, she turned around.

Gus walked down the steps and crossed the yard. She waited, her gaze taking him in as if might be a salesman or unwanted stranger. He unzipped his jacket for her to see the badge pinned on his shirt. Teddy looked back and made one of the joyful garbles of sounds he uttered when he saw someone he knew. She pointed to her mouth and shook her head. Gus nodded he understood.

159

Teddy leaned against her, and she held him close. She reached out her other hand, took Gus's in hers, and pressed it to her cheek. She smiled. Then she let go and stared at the sky again, as if Gus weren't there. As if this time it was Gus's turn to disappear.

Epilogue

Gus studied his seatbelt.

"Beautiful day for flying," the man in the window seat said.

Gus inserted one end into the buckle.

"Be dark, though, when we cross the mountains. Won't be able to see much."

"Not sure I want to," Gus said.

"Nervous?"

"A bit."

"First time?"

"It is," Gus said.

"Settle back and relax. These Lockheed Constellations are smooth as silk. Is L.A. your final destination?"

"I think so."

"You're not sure?"

"I'm meeting someone. I'm not sure what her plans are."

"When men don't know what they're doing, there's usually a *her* involved—somewhere, somehow. Three times I've been married. I speak from experience."

The door shut. The plane shook. The motors started. The stewardess explained emergency procedures. The plane taxied down the runway.

"What you put under the seat looks like a typewriter case."

"It is," Gus said.

The motors roared. The plane lifted into the sky.

"Just the case or is there a typewriter too?"

"There is."

"You're a writer then?"

"Not yet."

The man shook his head. "I suppose lugging a typewriter around keeps you fit."

"The woman I'm visiting asked me to bring it."

"They're available in California and newer than what you got, but she probably knows that."

"I like what I have."

"Old stuff, you mean?"

"What I'm used to."

"California might change your mind. Make a new man out of you."

"I think she's counting on it," Gus said.

A Mind *of* Winter

———∾∾∾———

The End

———∾∾∾———

Other books in the Gus Salt series

Book 1: *A Pinch of Salt*

ISBN: 978-0-9978686-8-5
$15.95

Book 2: *Percy's Field*

ISBN: 978-0-9978686-1-6
$15.95

Book 3: *Nolan's Cross*

ISBN: 978-0-9978686-3-0
$15.95

About the Author

CHRISTOPHER BROOKHOUSE is the author of several works of poetry and fiction, among them *Running Out*, which earned the Rosenthal Award from the American Academy of Arts & Letters; *A Selfish Woman*, nominated for the National Book Award; and *Fog, the Jeffrey stories*, winner of the biennial New Hampshire fiction prize.

A Mind of Winter is the final of his Gus Salt series, the first of which, *A Pinch of Salt*, was published in 2017. The second and third, *Percy's Field* and *Nolan's Cross*, were published in 2018 and 2019, respectively.